11/11

The Lovely Shoes

SUSAN SHREVE

ARTHUR A. LEVINE BOOKS

AN IMPRINT OF SCHOLASTIC INC.

new little wonders

Isaak and Henry and Aden and Padget

and to Aaron Jacobs

Text copyright © 2011 by Susan Shreve

Published by Arthur A. Levine Books, an imprint of Scholastic Inc.,
Publishers since 1920. SCHOLASTIC, the LANTERN LOGO, and associated logos are
trademarks and/or registered trademarks of Scholastic Inc.

Library of Congress Cataloging-in-Publication Data

Shreve, Susan Richards.
The lovely shoes / Susan Shreve. — 1st ed.   p.   cm.
Summary: In 1950s Ohio, ninth-grader Franny feels isolated and
self-conscious at high school because of her deformed leg and feet,
but her irrepressibly high-spirited mother is determined to find shoes
for Franny to wear at the school dances.

ISBN 978-0-439-68049-3 (hardcover : alk. paper)
[1. People with disabilities — Fiction.   2. Self-acceptance — Fiction.   3. Mothers and
daughters — Fiction.   4. High schools — Fiction.   5. Schools — Fiction.]
I. Title. PZ7.S55915Lp 2011 [Fic] — dc22   2010027937

10 9 8 7 6 5 4 3 2 1   11 12 13 14 15

First edition, June 2011

Printed in the U.S.A.   23

One

KISS THE GIMP

It was the night of the last dance at Easterbrook High, dusk, late June, and Franny Hall was looking out her bedroom window to check if choir practice had let out at St. James Episcopal Church next door.

No one was on the street except Mr. Goodly, walking his elderly basset hound in the front garden of the church.

Franny hurried down the stairs, checking herself in the mirror in the front hall, something she had been doing recently as if expecting a stranger reflected in the glass. That's how she sometimes felt, a stranger to her own self, and was almost surprised to see the same straight black hair in a ponytail, the same freckles and wide-set eyes she recognized as Francine Hall of Easterbrook, Ohio, U.S.A.

She opened the front door, calling to tell her mother that she was leaving.

"I'll be back by ten-thirty," she said.

An upstairs window flew open and Margaret Hall leaned out.

"Phone us to pick you up," her mother said. "I don't want you to walk home alone in the dark."

As if anything ever happened in Easterbrook, even in the dark.

"Things happen," her mother had said at dinner that night. "Especially at the high school dances."

By the time Franny reached the sidewalk, choir practice had let out and so she walked quickly, as quickly as she could under the circumstances, hoping to escape the choir boys in her class who had a habit of making fun of her.

Turning right at the end of her driveway, she headed in the direction of her cousin Eleanor's house, but too late. Already the boys had spilled onto the sidewalk — Andy Freeze and Tommy Wade loping by her, brushing against her shoulder as they passed, their hands in the pockets of their jeans.

"Franny Banany," Tommy said. "Heading to the dance?"

"I am. With Eleanor and Boots," Franny said, her stomach tightening, thinking she should have said nothing at all.

Don't give those silly boys the time of day, her mother would have told her.

"*Can* you dance, Franny?" Andy asked, laughter in his voice.

"I can dance," she said, anticipating remarks like that, especially from the boys. Not that they didn't like her — they liked her high spirits and giggly laugh. They even thought of her as funny and pretty, *pretty above the waist*, Randy Burns once said to her in his thoughtless way, as if to pretend he was giving her a compliment.

Randy Burns crashed into the group and the boys bumped up against one another like puppies, their arms flailing, bending over in uncontrollable hyena cries.

"Have fun, Franny Banany, and watch out for the senior boys."

The choir boys rushed ahead, turning off College Street, and Franny walked on alone, the street silent except for the low roar of cars in the distance, the only sound that of her left shoe hitting the sidewalk with a thump from the heavy lift she wore to even the length of her crippled left leg with her right one.

At the square she turned right on Scioto Street where her cousin Eleanor lived, passing the Sweet Shoppe on the corner lit up and crowded mostly with high school students already in their formal dresses and gathered outside, leaning against the glass. Several members of the Adorables, the eighth-grade girls club to which a lot of girls including Franny had *not* been invited to belong, were licking the tops of their double-dip ice-cream cones.

"Are you going tonight?" Belinda Rae asked as Franny passed by, not wishing to stop for conversation.

"I am," she said.

She didn't even ask if the Adorables were going to the dance. Of course they were.

"With your cousin?"

"Yes and also Boots."

"Cool," Belinda said. "Has anybody told you about the kissing contest?"

"I've heard about it," Franny said.

"We're planning to keep out of the way of that," Belinda Rae said, and the rest of the Adorables agreed.

"Me too," Franny said, although it had never occurred to her to worry.

Every year most of the girls in the eighth grade and a few of the boys went to the senior prom, not to the dance because they weren't invited, but to stand outside the Knights of Columbus Hall, peering in the windows, watching to see what would be in store for them when they went to high school. They carried cookies and thermoses of lemonade, and after they got bored watching the dancing inside the hall, they sat on the ground and whispered back and forth about the *hot* boys or the *creepy* ones, or danced on the lawn in front of the Knights of Columbus Hall to the music that wafted through the open windows onto the street. Some of the older boys broke the rules and brought liquor and drank it in the boys' room, and a few staggered out of the dance hall leaning against the building, falling over their own feet *drunk as skunks*, as her father described their behavior.

In the shadows of the building, couples wrapped around each other, and by ten o'clock most of the girls in the eighth grade had been picked up by their parents on Mission Avenue and driven home.

Stories traveled from one eighth-grade class to the next about the "kissing contest" during which one of the older boys was chosen to slip out the back door of the Knights of Columbus Hall, grab an eighth-grade girl, kiss her on the lips *really hard* as Eleanor had said, and run so quickly that no one would have a chance to see him well enough to identify in daylight. The kissing contest was a ritual repeated every year since anyone could remember, even when Franny's father, Dr. Henry Hall, had gone to Easterbrook High. According to stories, the kissing boy had never been caught and the girl chosen for kissing was immediately famous even before she started ninth grade.

It was a rite of passage that every girl in Easterbrook half wished and half feared would happen to her, including Franny Hall, who knew that she would never be the one chosen.

At the end of the square, just before Scioto Street branched off into Eleanor's neighborhood, Franny went into Grace's Variety to get presents for Eleanor and Boots, *little nothings* she called them, buying dollar packets of trading cards with the pictures of Hollywood actresses on the front. Franny was known for the presents she gave — bags of cookies or lollipops, costume jewelry from Grace's — to mark occasions like this one, the last year in elementary school, the first high school dance. She dropped the trading cards in her bag and headed down the street to the second block of Scioto, turning into the driveway of her cousin's house, where her best friend and sometime enemy Eleanor Hall was sitting on the front steps with Boots, Franny's other best friend.

Boots was wearing a little girl pale pink dress her mother had made for her to wear to the Catholic church on Sundays, and Eleanor had on a new lavender jumper with penny loafers and a puffed-sleeved blouse. From the pocket of her jumper, she rescued a tube of lipstick she had taken from her mother's dressing table and handed it to Franny.

"Apple red," she said.

"Great," Franny said. "I love everything red."

She dumped her bag and gave them their trading cards.

"Franny Claus," Boots said. "You give the best presents."

"June Allyson!" Eleanor exclaimed, flipping through the actress trading cards. "I don't have a June Allyson or an Ava Gardner or even Sophia Loren. This is so great, Franny."

"Don't give so many presents, darling," her mother had said too many times. "It worries me that you feel you need to buy presents."

"I don't need to buy presents," Franny had said. "I want to buy them."

And that was true. She did want to buy things for her friends. But deep down she also believed she *needed* to buy presents. Not that her friends didn't like her, but she couldn't escape a lingering fear she'd had since she could remember that she must work especially hard to keep their friendship.

"I thought you might change your mind and stay home," Eleanor said as Franny sat down on the steps.

"How come?"

"I just thought you might decide you didn't really like dances," Eleanor said.

"Well, I'm here," Franny said.

"So do I look okay?" Eleanor asked.

"You look like you always do, which is perfect," Franny said, easy with compliments.

"You too," Eleanor said.

"Not exactly perfect," Franny said cheerfully.

No one — certainly not Eleanor or Boots, who knew her better than anyone except her mother — would have guessed that Franny Hall had a moment of sadness, because she kept her real feelings to herself. Even from her mother and father and little brother, Ezekiel, called Zeke.

That was the kind of girl she was.

Crippled was how Franny's father, Dr. Henry Hall — who as the pediatrician for all the children in Easterbrook did not mince words — described Franny's condition. Even Margaret Hall, her amazing mother who seemed to be able to fix anything that went wrong, couldn't fix a leg and two feet that had been squished and twisted in Margaret Hall's belly before Franny was born, resulting in a *birth defect*, as her parents described the skinny little stick of flesh and bone that was her left leg, her damaged feet.

Margaret Hall was Franny's true best friend. In Easterbrook, they were a famous pair, mother and daughter flying on their bikes through the sleepy town as if they owned the streets. Margaret — tall, willowy, with black curly hair and a kind of daring surprising in the 1950s in a small Midwestern town — would ride her Schwinn around the square, where the shops were located, wearing short shorts and bare feet in the summer, long skirts and boots in the winter, with Zeke strapped into a seat on the back of the bike. Behind her, on a child's Schwinn, Franny, dressed like her mother in short shorts in summer and long skirts in winter, and always, winter and summer, heavy brown oxfords with a three-inch lift on the shoe of her skinny left leg.

Above the waist, Franny looked like a miniature version of her mother, long black hair but no curls, high cheekbones, wide-set eyes, *kissable lips*, her mother had told her.

"What does that mean?" Franny had asked.

"Just full, pretty lips," her mother had laughed. "Especially fetching on such a good, pure girl."

Goodness was what distinguished Franny.

"Good as gold," her father, who gave few compliments, said of her.

"Too good, darling," her mother had told her. "Too agreeable."

"I have to be agreeable," Franny said.

She knew that about herself but she believed she had no choice. It was her role to make people happy, to listen to their troubles as if she had no troubles herself, to give presents for the pleasure of it, to smile as if it made no difference when girls in the class whispered behind her back. *Agreeable* had worked for Franny so far, at least in elementary school.

Eleanor, leading the way to the Knights of Columbus Hall on the other side of the square, was walking just ahead of Boots and Franny, swinging her hips.

"I hope I'm *not* the girl kissed by one of the senior boys," she said, her head bobbing to the music already in the air on Main Street.

"It won't be me," Boots said. "My mother would kill me dead if any boy kissed me before I'm married."

Franny walked with Boots, her arm though hers, a light wind blowing her hair across her face, a little breathless, trying to keep up.

"What about you, Franny?"

"I've never thought about kissing," she said.

Which wasn't exactly true.

She had thought about kissing, sometimes at night when the lights in her room were out and the stars were bright over the steeple of St. James Episcopal Church and a sense of floating came over her, as if she belonged to a magical kingdom and the church was her palace and everywhere in the village, the young men desired her company.

But the actual fact of lips on her lips, of breath mixed with her breath, of that much closeness filled her with longing and dread.

The Adorables were already at the Knights of Columbus Hall when Franny arrived, standing on tiptoe, peering in the windows of the hall lit up with blinking lights.

"This is so fun," Eleanor said, standing with the Adorables. "I honestly can't wait for high school." She threw her arm around Franny's shoulder. "Can you?"

"Me neither," Franny agreed, although she actually hated change, hated the idea of leaving the warm cocoon of elementary school where she knew everyone and everyone knew her, where the teachers said she was the best-natured student in the class and very smart.

High school seemed like a war zone in which a girl like Franny could be in particular danger.

In the hot gym, they were fast dancing, the rock and roll and the jitterbug, which Franny had never tried, only watched on Friday nights when Eleanor and some of the girls in the eighth grade danced in her recreation room. She realized that she would *never* be able to fast dance. But after the lights dimmed and the music slowed to melody and the bodies swayed together like sails in a calm, that kind of dancing was possible for Franny, and she watched the couples, thinking of herself as one of them.

It was getting late, almost ten, and some of the older boys had wandered outside, large, thick boys, strangers, with spiked hair and low voices that rose to a kind of crescendo in the still spring air.

Franny was standing on the edge of the circle of eighth-grade girls who were dancing on the lawn, Eleanor dancing with Boots, the Adorables dancing with one another.

Randy Burns in a button-down dress shirt with the sleeves rolled up was standing by the front door, Randy's elbow resting on Tommy's shoulders. But most of the eighth-grade boys had stayed away, not up to the risk of embarrassing themselves in front of the older boys.

Tommy moved closer to Franny.

"I don't think I'm going to like high school," he said.

"How come?"

"Stuff like the kissing contest. So dumb! It hasn't happened yet, has it?"

"I don't think so." Franny was tentative.

The music inside was picking up, rising to the tempo of the next fast dance. The doors opened and several more boys came outside, shouting over one another's voices, the girls still dancing on the lawn.

Leaning against the building in the shadows next to the front door, Franny noticed a boy she had seen before, maybe at the Sweet Shoppe or coming from church, a tall, skinny boy with a Brylly wave of black hair plastered high on his forehead. He stood on the top step of the Knights of Columbus Hall, surveying the dancing on the lawn, one hand in his pocket. Something in the expression on his face, the way he looked at the girls dancing, a certain curling of his lips as if he were chuckling to himself alarmed Franny. She stepped back, away from the light that spread across the lawn from the double doors, away from Tommy

Wade, and before she even had a chance to catch herself in the dark, she had fallen backward.

The boy must have seen her fall and taken a leap from the top step to the ground, rushing into the center of the eighth-grade girls, grabbing one of the Adorables, grabbing her around the waist, kissing her hard on the lips, and as he headed on his escape route around the building, passing Franny who was struggling up from the ground where she had fallen, he leaned over, mumbling under his breath, "Kiss the gimp!"

And then he disappeared into the darkness.

Franny scrambled to her feet, brushed the dirt off, her breath caught in her throat.

"So, was it fun?" Margaret asked after she had dropped Eleanor and Boots at their own houses and she and Franny were in the car alone.

"It was fun," Franny said. "Fun enough."

"And did you dance?"

"I danced with the girls on the lawn outside, with Boots and Eleanor. But slow dancing. I can't do fast."

"You'll learn. We'll practice together." Her mother turned into the driveway, pulled up the brake, turned off the engine.

"And can you imagine what it will be like next year at the high school dances? Can you imagine yourself in a new formal gown, your hair swept up, maybe with flowers?"

"Of course, I can imagine it," Franny said, glad it was dark in the car, that her mother couldn't see her face or hear the thumping of her beating heart.

What she couldn't imagine was telling her mother about the boy who whispered *gimp* in her ear. That would break her mother's heart.

"High school will be great," she said. "I can't wait."

WISHFUL THINKING

Franny stood in front of the full-length mirror on the door to her mother's closet, examining her feet. In spite of a cold winter wind blowing through the cracks of the Halls' old Victorian house, she was wearing very little — her Carter's cotton underwear, a black strapless bra borrowed from Eleanor, and her mother's blue satin high-heeled shoes, one of sixty-seven pairs of shoes stacked on the shelves of the closet, some of them with the price tag still stuck to the bottom.

If she held on to the closet door to keep her balance in the narrow, spiky shoes so she wouldn't tumble when her left leg gave out — then her feet, hidden in the blue satin shoes, looked almost normal, like the feet of a regular fourteen-year-old girl, small for her age.

The blue satins were Franny's favorite of her mother's shoes. The toe round like the toes of the patent leather Mary Janes she'd never been able to wear as a child, the heel wide at the top thinning to the width of a pencil, and the satin the pure blue of summer skies.

In the next room, her mother was talking as usual with her aunt Estelle about the problems Franny was having in the ninth grade. *Trials and tribulations* were her mother's words for problems and that afternoon the subject was the Valentine's Dance.

"I *don't* have problems," Franny had told her mother in the first weeks of ninth grade at Easterbrook High.

"But you're not like your old self," her mother said.

"Maybe I'm getting a new self to fit high school," Franny had said lightly, but she didn't want to talk to her mother about her daily life, not the way she used to talk to Margaret about almost everything.

It was February, the kind of sullen, gray day that colored every winter afternoon in northwest Ohio, and the snow, already dirty with soot, was banked up to the front porch.

"Franny and I are going to Cleveland this afternoon to buy a formal dress for the dance," her mother was saying to Estelle, full of her usual high spirits.

As if Franny would ever be willing to go to a formal dance in the gymnasium of Easterbrook High.

She had worried about high school dances ever since the night at the Knights of Columbus Hall, when she'd fallen in the dark and the phantom boy had leaned over, whispering in her face.

Sometimes unable to sleep, a general agitation spinning her brain like a top, she lay in bed thinking of what she might have said to him, what she might have done, her back stiffening, her arms tight, ready to swing at the air.

"I can't go to school dances," Franny had said in October after the first dance at the high school. "I look too stupid in the shoes I have to wear."

"We'll fix it," Margaret Hall had said.

"You can't fix it!" Franny said. "This problem is permanent."

"I will find a way."

"Don't bother," Franny said, occasionally bad-tempered since she'd started ninth grade, bothered by her friends at school, irritated by her mother's irrepressible high spirits.

"I only want you to be happy," Margaret Hall said.

"I *am* happy," Franny said sharply, a burning in her throat. It made her ill on the rare occasions she was angry at her mother, who wanted more than anything for Franny to be *normal*, to have a life like every other girl in Easterbrook, Ohio, to grow up and go to college and marry a man who lived maybe in New York City or

Chicago or San Francisco, some big city close to an ocean or a lake so Margaret could visit her there.

Franny did not believe she would ever be normal. That was her life as she saw it, no matter how much her mother wished it could be different.

Thanksgiving had been at Eleanor's house that year with all the Hall family gathered in the dining room as they did every Thanksgiving, either at Eleanor's house or Franny's, sitting at the long candlelit table with too much food and conversation about Easterbrook and the neighbors and what the children were doing that year, the grown-ups talking and talking, the children wishing for dessert. When the subject of high school came up, the dishes had been cleared, the pies lined up in front of Aunt Gabbie, Eleanor's unpleasant mother, Zeke sleeping, his face against the starchy tablecloth.

"So, Franny." Aunt Gabbie began cutting the dreadful mincemeat pie. "I understand that you're not very happy at Easterbrook High School."

"Well, Gabbie," Margaret broke in quickly. "Not that Franny isn't happy . . ."

"That's just what I heard from Eleanor." Gabbie passed a plate of pie. "Small or large mincemeat, Franny?"

"Neither," Franny said.

"We have apple as well."

"No, thank you."

"Franny . . ." Margaret began.

"If she doesn't want pie, she doesn't want pie. It's not a requirement," her father said, but already Franny had gotten up from the table, put her napkin down, and glanced at Zeke in the hope that he might follow her, but he was still sleeping.

She walked out of the dining room, down the hall to the vestibule, and before anyone at the table realized that she had not left to go to the bathroom, she had opened the front door.

Her mother caught up with her halfway down the block.

"Franny, what are you doing?"

"I'm going home."

"But what about dinner, darling?"

"I finished dinner, I hate Aunt Gabbie's pies, and I hate Aunt Gabbie."

She continued walking.

"I'll come with you then."

"I don't want you to come with me," Franny said with

a certainty that surprised her. "If the subject comes up again, I am perfectly happy in high school."

Franny closed the closet door in her parents' bedroom and flopped on their bed, facedown.

She had no interest in the Valentine's Dance. Or even in Valentine's Day since she didn't have a boyfriend to declare his love forever with a tiny box of Whitman's chocolate-covered cherries or a lacy valentine with *"I love you, a bushel and a peck / A bushel and a peck and a hug around the neck. . . ."*

By the time a girl got to freshman year in Easterbrook, Ohio, a boyfriend was necessary. All the girls that Franny knew, except Boots and Eleanor, had boyfriends. Each Monday morning a new couple would arrive at the high school building holding hands, hooking up the night before on the telephone or at the counter of the Sweet Shoppe or the cemetery where the high school students met to make out. By recess that day, the freshmen would serenade the new couple on the grassy hill behind the school, singing, *"Tom and Sylvie, sittin' in a tree, k-i-s-s-i-n-g / First comes love, then comes marriage, then comes Sylvie with a baby carriage."*

Franny had no one. Not this year. Maybe not ever.

Every other girl in the ninth grade except maybe Boots had been thinking about the Valentine's Dance since the morning after the Christmas Dance, which Franny didn't attend.

Even Esther Sams came to the dances in leg braces from polio and sat on the sidelines, and Chrissy Freemont who had no friends at all, neither boys nor girls, was there, and Betsy Frame who was so enormous, she was likely to fall on her face if she tried to dance.

"Let's go to the Valentine's Dance together," Eleanor had said.

Franny shook her head.

"I don't like dances."

"But maybe if we go as a group."

"I hate the way I look."

"I hate the way I look." She said it again to her mother one winter afternoon sitting in the kitchen drinking hot chocolate with whipped cream.

"You're going to be beautiful, Franny," Margaret Hall said, as if "going to be" meant anything to Franny *now*.

Franny rolled her eyes.

"You're very pretty now but you will be beautiful. No one gets to be beautiful until she is older and wiser."

"And when is that?"

"Soon," her mother said. "I promise."

The problem for Franny was how she *felt*, which was self-conscious, as if everyone at Easterbrook High was passing judgment.

Her mother *was* beautiful. Sometimes Franny's breath caught in her throat just watching Margaret Hall fly around the kitchen making dinner, her black curls laced with perspiration, half-glasses balancing on her nose just beneath her wide-set silver-blue eyes, clicking across the linoleum floor in high, high heels, her calves perfectly curved.

Margaret Hall was Danish, born in Copenhagen where she grew up with her older sister, Estelle. She might even have married her boyfriend in Copenhagen and had Danish children instead of Franny and Zeke if it were not for a year she spent in New York City when she was eighteen, living with Estelle and Estelle's American husband, Uncle Douglas.

But that year in New York City turned into twenty after she met Franny's father, Henry Hall, on a snowy

December evening waiting for the uptown Lexington Avenue subway. Dr. Henry Hall had swished his Danish sweetheart back to his hometown of Easterbrook, in the corner of Ohio where he had grown up and planned to spend the rest of his life taking care of Easterbrook's children.

"If I had not left Copenhagen in the first place, I never would have had you, my joy," her mother used to say to Franny when she was young.

"Or Zeke either," Franny would add and her mother would nod her head.

Zeke, born eight years after Franny, was an angel of a boy with cherry red cheeks and yellow hair. "Easy as pie, my Zeke," Margaret would say of her little boy. "Sugar and spice and everything nice, just like a girl, only he's not one."

She didn't mean for Franny to feel bad about the perfect Zeke but in her secret heart, Franny knew she had been a "problem" ever since she was born at Mercy Hospital at four in the morning on January 1, 1942.

It was 1956 and Franny had turned fourteen on New Year's Day. General Eisenhower was president of the United States and most of the girls she knew were in love with Elvis Presley. Even Franny practiced sticking out one hip bone, opening her mouth just so, half closing her eyes, and in the lowest register possible belting out *"Love me tender / Love me sweet / Never let me go."* There was an Elvis fan club at Easterbrook High called the Real Gone Teen Gals, and Boots had joined and even Eleanor. People in Easterbrook were convinced the Americans would be blown up by the Russians, but Margaret Hall, who knew more about war since she had grown up in Denmark next door to Germany before the Second World War, had said that no one would be blowing up Ohio any time soon.

People's lives in Easterbrook were ordinary, even dull, and the only trouble that Franny could remember that year was the time Boots's brother Blue drove his father's car into La Mama's Italian Restaurant on Christmas Day.

Easterbrook was located on Route 46 halfway between Toledo and Cleveland, not close enough to either city to be anything but a blip on the Ohio map, surrounded by farmland with houses so far off the road you might think only cows lived there, and communities of Amish families who traveled the roads in their horse-drawn buggies but mainly stuck to themselves. The Halls lived in a large white clapboard house with turrets and shutters and a wraparound front porch at the end of College Street next to the Episcopal church.

Nothing of particular interest happened to capture the attention of a high-tempered girl like Franny Hall except church on Sundays, which the Halls did not attend, and high school couples making out on Friday nights behind the tombstones at the Oakdale Cemetery, and dances after the football or basketball or baseball games, depending on the season.

And occasionally, Saturday trips to Cleveland to shop in the department stores.

On this Saturday morning, it was beginning to look as if Franny would be going on the Greyhound bus to Cleveland as soon as her mother hung up the telephone with Aunt Estelle.

Franny put the blue satin high heels back on the shelf, slipped down the corridor, past Zeke's room where he was lying on his back playing with race cars on his belly, past the office where her mother was still talking on the phone, to her own bedroom where she pulled the door *almost* shut.

"You can't find a dress worth wearing in Easterbrook," Margaret Hall was saying to Estelle as Franny put her ear to the crack in the door.

"She doesn't want to go to the dance because of her shoes," her mother said after a pause, "but maybe she will change her mind if we find a remarkable dress, long enough to cover her feet."

Franny could imagine Aunt Estelle's reply. Sensible Estelle, less beautiful than Franny's mother, less patient with children and much less fun, would click her tongue against the roof of her mouth, clear her throat like she did when she wanted to say something important, and in a low, judgmental tone of voice, would remark, "If Francine won't go to the dance in the shoes she's got, that's her choice."

The shoes to which Aunt Estelle would have been referring were the high-top brown orthopedic oxfords that Franny had worn every day of her life since she could remember, the kind that babies wear to support their tiny ankles while they are learning to walk. Franny's shoes were so wide and clunky that they hid the evidence of her crippled foot, which looked a little like a sand crab when Franny walked barefoot.

"Not to worry about funny little feet," her mother had told her. "Everyone has some kind of adversity — a little of this is wrong, a little of that. Something troubling comes in every life. Like Aunt Estelle has teeth like the teeth of a dinosaur and Daddy lost some of the sight in his left eye and I have asthma which gets worse in cold, damp Ohio."

When she was small, Franny had actually believed what her mother said about the fair distribution of problems, imagining that God sitting in his heavenly chair was distributing bad news like Halloween candy, one for you and one for you and one for you. So she considered herself lucky not to be profoundly deaf like Alyssa Burns in the grade below her or stained by a beige birthmark on her cheek like Sue Ellen Laster. Things happened to people, good and bad, was what she used to think, just like her mother had told her.

In elementary school, Franny had even been one of the *liked* girls, not too smart or too girly or too much of a teacher's pet. Not a teacher's pet at all. Just a funny, high-spirited, happy-go-lucky kind of girl with a heart patch on her jeans, a high ponytail, and clunky leather shoes that she wore like a badge of honor. You could hear her coming when she walked the corridors of the elementary school.

Everyone in town knew Franny Hall, whether they *really* knew her or not. At least they knew who she was, the girl with mismatched legs who walked with a hitch in her gait so her hips twirled.

And for a while that felt like *popular* to Franny.

Things began to change *for real*, as Zeke would say, as soon as she started ninth grade at Easterbrook High School. One Monday in October, the week of the Harvest Dance, she had arrived at school, surprised to find the rest of her homeroom clustered in the hall talking about the dance. She hesitated, wondering whether to join the group, when Sandy Frost turned to her and said in an aside but loud enough for others near her to hear: "Going to the dance, Franny?" and before she had a chance to answer, Sandy replied for her, saying, "I guess it'd be too hard for you to dance."

"I can dance fine," Franny said. "I'm not coming for other reasons."

She leaned against the wall, light-headed, tears stinging just behind her eyelids, waiting for a chance to slip away unnoticed from the group of girls before the others realized her feelings had been hurt.

Sitting in the back row of homeroom, pretending to write in her composition book, she wished she had said nothing at all, simply passed by Sandy Frost as if she had heard her question but it wasn't worth answering, as if Sandy didn't even exist. During recess, she had gone to the library, turning the pages of *Huckleberry Finn* without really looking at the words. At the end of classes, she stopped in the girls' room and waited until everyone else had left school for the Sweet Shoppe or the drugstore soda fountain and then walked home the back way along Allison Road. Twice during the next week, she'd gone to the infirmary with a threatened stomach flu that never materialized.

She didn't mention high school to her mother. She didn't need to.

"You don't seem to like high school," her mother said wistfully one evening after dinner as they were drying dishes in the kitchen. "At least not in the way you used to like school when you came home bubbling with news."

"I like it well enough," Franny said. "But I don't like dances."

"I wish you'd *try*. You will look so lovely in a gown. Sometimes I lie in bed at night thinking about you with your black hair, in a long silvery blue dress, maybe strapless."

Franny could imagine her mother staring out the window of her study, where she worked as an illustrator for medical books, drawing intricate pictures of the inside layers of a human body and thinking of her only daughter in a long silk gown — Margaret called them gowns, not dresses — Franny's black hair piled on her head in a loose bun, dancing in the arms of a handsome boy.

Tall and handsome, sometimes *tall, dark, and handsome* was the description Margaret Hall gave of every man she liked, including Henry Hall, who was not particularly handsome, although boyish — "cute" her cousin Eleanor said of Dr. Hall, but certainly not dark — his hair laced with gray, his complexion ruddy.

Lying in her bed next to the window overlooking the back garden and the steeple of St. James Episcopal Church, the lights out, the night bright with stars, Franny could also imagine herself in a long strapless dress, probably periwinkle blue, her black hair in curls done by Ethel's Hairstylist on Main Street, dancing in the arms of Mikey Houston.

SILVER SHOES

Franny sat in the front seat next to her mother on a Greyhound bus, traveling the highway to Cleveland. It had started to snow. She loved to travel with her mother, loved sitting next to her, watching the pleasure on the faces of passengers boarding the bus in the small towns between Easterbrook and Cleveland when they saw Margaret Hall, thinking how beautiful she was, how elegant, dressed off the pages of fashion magazines.

That particular day, her mother was wearing black trousers and a tight black crewneck sweater, with a red silk square tied around her neck. Her hair, dark like Franny's but curly, with a white stripe across the front — *dyed* white. "Skunk fashion," Margaret said. None of the women in Easterbrook wore trousers, probably not even the women in Cleveland, and no one dyed her hair unless it had already turned gray, which Margaret's had not. On that Saturday, she was wearing a gray fedora, her favorite of the many hats she owned, and even in trousers, she wore very high heels, red ones to match the red scarf. No makeup except mascara. She never wore lipstick.

Two seats back, Mrs. Arnold Clifford, the grandmother of Lucia in Franny's class, and Miss Esther Clifford, the grown-up, unmarried daughter with whom Mrs. Clifford lived on North Main in Easterbrook, were chatting about Margaret Hall. Franny had seen them when she got on the bus and said hello and they had smiled *an Episcopalian smile*, as her mother would have described it, the kind of unnatural smile you *have* to give whether you're glad to see someone or not.

Franny held her breath so she could hear them above the low roar of the bus. Gossip was serious entertainment in Easterbrook, chatting back and forth about other people in town.

"Not enough happens in Easterbrook, so people need to talk about each other," her mother had told Franny.

"Margaret comes from Copenhagen," Mrs. Clifford was saying.

"I know, Mother," Miss Esther Clifford said. "That's why she dresses in pants the way she does."

"Women do that in Copenhagen."

"And she doesn't go to church. I see her on her front porch reading the paper every Sunday morning when we walk to church, even in the winter. Have you noticed?" Miss Clifford asked.

"I've noticed," Mrs. Clifford said. "People in Denmark don't believe in God. At least that's what I've heard. They may believe in *something* but certainly not in Christianity."

"I read in *National Geographic* that Scandinavia is very liberal," Miss Clifford agreed.

Franny turned to her mother, who had a funny smile on her face.

"Say something to them," Franny whispered.

Margaret put her finger to her lips.

"But it's not true what they're saying," Franny said.

"It's not important what they're saying."

Margaret was counting her money, $127.50 from the stash she kept in her underwear drawer for luxuries. She saved the money she made from the medical books she illustrated for unnecessary things, luxuries like formal dresses for the Valentine's Dance or the rhinestone drop earrings she was wearing on the trip to Cleveland.

"I have saved up quite a lot for us to spend this afternoon," she said.

The bus stopped in Gainesville to pick up passengers, a boy about eighteen, a young man, a mother with a baby.

Franny was aware that they were looking at her mother as they walked down the aisle of the bus. People did. She could feel their eyes. The young man staring at Margaret Hall stopped next to them, put his hand on the seat in front for balance when the bus started up.

"You look just like this girl I had a crush on at Wooster," he said. "Mary Jo Rider."

"That's not me," Margaret said and she was smiling. "And I'm a lot older than you are."

"Well, I'd never guess," the man said, and he would have stayed there trying to make conversation if the bus driver had not asked him to please take a seat.

"So it's fifty percent off regular prices in the formal gown section on the third floor of Marcus and Sons department store," Margaret said, tearing the ad out of the Saturday edition of the *Cleveland Plain Dealer*. "We can get two or even three dresses with the money I've saved. You'll need one dress for spring and one for winter. Maybe I'll even buy one."

"I'm not necessarily going to the Valentine's Dance, Mama," Franny said softly, choosing the word *necessarily* with care, knowing how important her happiness was to her mother and not wishing to disappoint her, especially after she had saved all that money.

"But if you do decide at the last minute to go to the dance, then you'll have the perfect dress, darling, and if you decide no, then we've had a lovely day in Cleveland together."

Franny looked out the window at the passing farms, the thin sheet of snow, the bare trees bending just so with the wind.

"I have so many dreams for you, Franny," her mother whispered conspiratorially. "And now that you're almost grown-up, some of them will come true."

"I know," Franny replied, her heart heavy just thinking of all those dreams bearing down on her like heat.

Not that she felt hopeless about her life. She had dreams too, about her future with Mikey Houston and turning into someone important, like an orthopedic surgeon taking care of crippled children like her.

Unlike her mother, her father expected very little of Franny's romantic future. He was a brusque, straightforward man without illusions.

"A doctor has to tell the truth," he said, "and that's what I do."

"Marriage isn't for everyone," he'd tell Franny when her mother spun magical possibilities for her life. "You'll be wise to find a profession."

When her father advised Franny to find a profession, she understood him to mean that it was possible no one would *want* to marry her.

"Don't be such a pessimist, Henry," her mother had said to him crossly.

"I'm a realist, Margaret," her father said. "And you're an optimist."

"I'm sorry your father is so difficult," her mother said later that evening.

"It's okay. That's the way he is," Franny said.

The girls in Franny's class at Easterbrook were at war with their mothers sometime between elementary and high school, as if at the end of eighth grade, mothers took a bitter pill that turned them into monsters. Even Boots's mother, who taught seventh-grade history and English and had a reputation for being the best teacher at Easterbrook Elementary, transformed overnight into an agent of pain inflicting misery on her daughters, particularly Boots.

"What's the matter with her?" Franny asked.

"Mothers get to be annoying like they've caught a disease." Boots shrugged. "I hate the way she talks in that teacher voice. It sends shivers down my spine."

"It hasn't happened to me with my mother."

"Don't hold your breath hoping for something different," Boots said, listing a litany of maternal sins.

Marianna Ward's mother wouldn't let her go to the movies and Joanne Bird's mother had actually belted Joanne for kissing Paul Clement at the entrance to Oakdale Cemetery in full view of the passing traffic and Brigette hadn't spoken to her mother for seven weeks as of February first, which included Christmas Day.

"It'll happen to you too," Boots said.

The bus crossed the city limits into Cleveland, and Margaret Hall took down her coat and put it on, wrapped a red woolly scarf around her neck.

"We're almost there," she said, handing Franny her coat.

At the first stop in downtown Cleveland, Miss Clifford and Mrs. Clifford got off, patting Franny on the head as they passed.

"Why, Margaret," Mrs. Clifford said as she angled her ample hips down the aisle, "you look so fashionable today."

"Going clothes shopping?" Miss Clifford asked, and she didn't mean it nicely.

"No, actually, we have friends in Cleveland," Margaret said, not willing to let the Clifford family in on her shopping plans. "Relatives from Copenhagen where I grew up."

"I wasn't aware that you had grown up in Copenhagen," Miss Clifford said, and Franny gave her mother a knowing look. "Very nice place to grow up, yes?"

"Very interesting," Mrs. Clifford added. "I haven't gotten to Copenhagen yet in my travels, but I plan to go maybe this summer."

And they stepped off the bus with a little wave, the doors closing behind them.

"I don't think Mrs. Clifford has traveled beyond Cleveland," Margaret said, standing for the next stop, which was Marcus and Sons.

Franny followed her mother, weaving in and out of the Saturday crowds and through the revolving doors into the store.

"So first to the third-floor formal dress sale," Margaret said.

Marcus and Sons was a huge department store, covering two city blocks with seven floors, from makeup on the ground floor to furniture on the seventh and an elegant restaurant on the second floor where Franny and her mother always ordered fruit cup with a maraschino cherry, a toasted cheese sandwich with a sour pickle, and maybe chocolate marshmallow ice cream with a macaroon for dessert.

"Why did you tell Miss Clifford we were visiting friends in Cleveland?" Franny asked as they were going up the escalator side by side.

"Because . . ." Margaret Hall paused. "I didn't want them going back to Easterbrook tut-tutting about our shopping trip."

"Is there something wrong with shopping?"

"They would think it's frivolous," her mother said, linking her arm through Franny's.

It surprised Franny when her mother told what she called a *white lie*, a small lie of convenience to avoid trouble. She thought of her mother as fearless — at least she wished to think of her as fearless, but it was her father, her serious, sometimes gloomy and severe father, who always told the literal truth.

"What I mean by one dress for winter and one for spring," Margaret Hall was saying, hurrying through the third floor to formal dresses, "is that your winter dress, maybe purple velvet or even black, is perfect for Christmas through February."

"I'm NOT going to dances," Franny said with sudden irritation.

Her mother laughed.

"Don't worry. You don't *have* to go to any dances. This is half pretend just for the fun of it," she went on. "Maybe a black velvet strapless?"

"And black mascara," Franny added. "I'd like to do something with my bushy eyebrows so they look bold like Audrey Hepburn's."

"Perfect," her mother said, leaning against Franny as they rode up the wooden escalator to the third floor. "I think I'd like to get extra thick mascara and we'll share."

In the dressing room, Franny sat on a Victorian arm chair with a puffy brocade seat, avoiding the image of herself reproduced in triplicate in the three-way mirror.

Hanging on a hook were the dresses her mother had picked from the lines of sale items on the rack.

"An A-line red velvet tea-length," she said. "What do you think?"

"Okay," Franny replied, less resistant when she saw the dresses accumulated on the hooks in the dressing room, wishing it was time for lunch.

"And this glittery taffeta, kind of a brownish gold, for fall probably, also strapless though I could make some little sleeves."

"It's okay."

"I think you're big enough to hold this dress up so it doesn't slip down to your waist."

Margaret had picked out a royal blue silk with a straight skirt, a V-neck, and cap sleeves. She held it up next to Franny.

"The color's great with your hair, but maybe the dress is too old for you with these little sleeves, and I don't know about a straight skirt."

Franny slipped out of her skirt and crewneck sweater, took off the high-top orthopedic shoes with the hunky lift, and kicked them out of the way.

"Remember, it doesn't *mean* anything if I try this thing on," she warned, expecting that whatever she said would make no difference. They would still leave the midwinter sales with two formal dresses — one for spring and one for winter. Her mother would never give up.

"Just in case you change your mind about the dance," her mother said, crossing her long legs.

Franny tried on the red velvet first. $25.00 marked down from $37.50.

"Too big." Margaret tilted her head to the side.

She helped Franny into a pink taffeta dress with a tulip skirt and a strapless cornflower blue thing with boning in the bra that jabbed Franny's ribs and made her stick out like the pointy end of an ice-cream cone.

A saleswoman knocked on the door, holding a hanger with a long black velvet strapless dress.

"Maybe this one?" she asked.

Margaret took the dress and held it in front of her, eyeing herself in the mirror.

"Try it on," she said, handing it to Franny.

"Aren't I too young for black?"

"It's very grown-up but maybe," Margaret said.

Franny stood in front of the long three-way mirror while her mother zipped the dress up the back, pulled her hair into a high bun, brushed her bangs so they fell in a swoop across her forehead, removed a magenta flower from one of the dresses on the hook, and with a bobby pin attached the flower just above Franny's ear, a splash of color on black.

"Oh, Franny, you look just beautiful!"

In the mirror, she looked at herself straight on. Everyone had always told Franny that she was going to look like her mother when she grew up, and this time seeing her mother reflected behind her, Franny could see her own future in the glass.

And her heart leapt.

"I think I like it," she said.

At home that afternoon, Zeke was sitting on his parents' bed, his Matchbox cars stuffed under the pillow where Pickle, the cat, was sleeping. He watched his sister walk across the room in the black velvet dress.

"Gorgeous, don't you think, Zekey?" Margaret asked.

"S'okay," Zeke said. "I mean, I don't know how Franny's supposed to look."

"Do I look like I'm limping?"

"You always limp, Franny," Zeke said truthfully. "That's how you walk."

"A little limp," Margaret Hall said. "Not noticeable."

"That's not true. It is noticeable," Franny said. "It's always noticeable. Right, Zekey?"

"Right," Zeke said, zooming his car up the wall.

"Well." Margaret Hall began as she often did with a pause. She was sitting in an armchair, her feet on the bed, a familiar expression Franny recognized on her face.

"Franny," she said softly, almost a whisper.

"What's the matter?"

"I have a plan."

Eldridges Shoes and Trinkets on the main square of Easterbrook was just about to lock the doors to business at five o'clock when Franny and Margaret and an unhappy Zeke Hall walked in.

"We're about to close, Mrs. Hall." Miss Fritchie, the store owner, looked up from the cash register. "You can come back on Monday when we open at ten."

Franny's mother leaned over the counter, touching Miss Fritchie very lightly on the wrist.

"I need your help, Miss Fritchie," she said. "I see you have a sale on shoes."

"We do, Mrs. Hall, but it's five o'clock."

"I know, Miss Fritchie, but Franny has no shoes for the Valentine's Dance next weekend."

"I don't know whether we have anything here that will work for Franny," Miss Fritchie said.

"We got a beautiful dress in Cleveland this morning and I hate to think of her in those heavy oxfords with a gorgeous black velvet dress. Strapless. I'm going to lend her my pearls."

Miss Fritchie was softening.

"I'll be very quick," Margaret Hall said.

Franny stepped onto the X-ray machine to look at the bones of her feet through the X-ray lens which showed bones without flesh. She stood on the rectangular box, used to measure the size of the feet exactly, stuck her feet into the two holes, turned on the machine, and peered through a window at the top of the box. She already knew that she had one foot that fit into a size five women's shoe and another foot that fit into a size thirteen children's shoe.

"If you can hurry, I'll stay open a few more minutes," Miss Fritchie said, closing the cash register.

"It's not my idea to be here in the first place," Franny said pleasantly as Miss Fritchie hurried past the X-ray machine on her way to lock the front door.

"Me neither," Zeke agreed, sitting glumly on the floor.

Margaret was searching through the shoes to find one size five and one size four, since the manufacturers didn't make high heels in children's size thirteen.

"Let's try these," her mother said, rolling up the pants leg of Franny's blue jeans, fitting her little foot into the smaller shoe.

Zeke had climbed onto the X-ray box and turned it on but he was too short to look down at his own feet in the box.

"That shoe is too big," Franny said.

"Of course it's too big."

"So?"

"So watch this."

Margaret took a package of Kleenex out of her purse, wadded up a bunch of it, and stuck it in the toe of the shoe.

"Now try it."

"It's still too big," Franny said, losing patience.

"There," Margaret said, adding a few more tissues. "Now stand up and see if you can walk."

"She doesn't want to do it, Mama," Zeke said.

Franny had never walked in high-heeled shoes, even ones with very small heels like the pair she was wearing.

"I'd have fallen over in those blue satin shoes of yours I tried on this morning," she said to warn her mother that she might fall over now.

"You won't fall," Margaret said, getting up from the floor, leaning against the wall, folding her arms across her chest.

"I want to go home," Zeke said, turning off the machine. "I couldn't see my feet."

But Margaret wasn't listening.

"They're very pretty shoes, darling. Pretty on you."

Franny took a step and then another. The heels were short and though she'd never walked in any shoes but orthopedic ones with the big lift, she was actually walking across the hardwood floor at Eldridges, and the shoes felt surprisingly fine. Not perfect and she *was* limping even more than usual, but the left shoe stuffed with Kleenex wasn't falling off and the right one felt almost normal. She looked at her feet in the square mirror on the floor of the shop.

Maybe, she thought, *the shoes would work just for a short time, a couple of hours, long enough to last the dance.*

She walked to the end of the store and back.

Miss Fritchie was putting on her winter coat and galoshes.

"Okay," she agreed. "I'll try it even though I hate silver shoes."

"I hate shopping," Zeke said.

She sat down on the bench, took the shoes off, took out the Kleenex, and examined them. The price marked on the sole was $5.95.

"Have a nice time at the dance," Miss Fritchie said, dropping the shoes, one pair size four and one pair size five, in a bag, unlocking the door for them to leave.

"Maybe I will," Franny said.

And maybe not, she thought.

But in spite of herself, in spite of her worries and better judgment, she was picturing herself in a black velvet strapless dress long enough to cover her feet hidden in silver shoes. She would be leaning against a post at the gymnasium, one hand on her hip, her eyes half closed in make-believe boredom, the expression she'd seen on the faces of the models in her mother's fashion magazines. The band would be playing Frank Sinatra's "In the Wee Small Hours of the Morning," the lights dim, and Mikey Houston would be moving across the gymnasium floor in Franny's direction.

THE 1956
EASTERBROOK HIGH
VALENTINE'S DANCE

The gymnasium at Easterbrook was a blaze of light, festooned with ribbons and strips of white crepe paper and flashing Christmas tree bulbs and pots of ferns and flowers. A huge red heart with two chairs decked out as thrones for the king and queen of the Valentine's Dance was at center stage, next to where Johnny and the Teddy Bears were playing "No Not Much."

Franny, her stomach on fire, walked into the gym with Boots.

Johnny was the lead singer, and his voice quivered and trilled as he sang to some girl that he didn't want his arms around her, but then admitted that wasn't true: *"Nnnnnnno, nnnnot, muuuuuuch."*

Franny wrapped her arms around her chest, determined to hold up her strapless black velvet dress. Her feet hurt in the silver shoes in spite of the toilet paper bed into which they'd been stuffed. But the pain, the simple physical pain in her fragile feet, didn't bother her so much as the possibility that she would humiliate herself right there in the gym with most of the people her age in the town of Easterbrook dancing their hearts out!

Boots was wearing a white dress with a gathered skirt and puffed sleeves.

"Because I'm Catholic and Catholics can't wear strapless."

Boots's parents had only permitted her to attend the Valentine's Dance if she wore a dress that looked very much like the dress she had worn when she was eight for her first Communion. They had a habit of worrying there could be *sex* at the dances and then Boots would be *defiled* and no one, at least no good Catholic boy, would want to marry her.

"I'd like to be defiled," Eleanor said. "Soon, while I'm still a freshman."

"Me too," Boots said. "And so would Franny, right Franny?"

Franny had thought about lying in her bed in the dark with Mikey Houston so he couldn't see her crippled foot, but she never wanted any boy to see her without all of her clothes. Defiled sounded similar to naked.

Marriage was the goal in Easterbrook, the only solution for a girl. Parents started to talk about their daughter's domestic future early, sometimes as early as eighth grade when coupling began at the soda shop. Boots's parents especially talked about her future as a wife and mother as if it might happen any moment.

"I'm so excited I can hardly stand it," Boots said. "Aren't you?"

"Not yet," Franny said.

She had started feeling sick at dinner.

"You feel sick because you're nervous," Dr. Henry Hall said. "I can give you a medical description of why your stomach reacts to nerves."

Her father liked to supply the family with medical information, what it meant when Franny's heartbeat accelerated or she blushed or Zeke sneezed as he was in the habit of doing or Margaret Hall had an asthma attack.

"No medical descriptions, thank you," Franny said.

"You'll be fine, in any case," Dr. Hall said.

"I feel sick too," Zeke said.

"You always feel what Franny is feeling, Zekey," Dr. Hall said. "You need to learn to feel for yourself."

"I do," Zeke said. "I feel sick."

Franny's mother leaned over and whispered in her ear. "You don't have to eat a thing, puss, whatever your father says. He doesn't understand girls or dances."

All week her mother had been teaching her to dance, especially slow dance, pushing the furniture in the living room against the wall, turning the Victrola on full volume.

Franny had a tendency to trip over her own feet.

"I can't do it," she said. "Especially I can't do the cheek-to-cheek dancing like you and Daddy do."

"We'll practice one more time in your bare feet before you put on your new shoes," her mother said.

Her mother put "Don't Fence Me In" on the Victrola, took Franny in her arms, and they danced as they had done the night before.

"I keep feeling as if I'm going to trip," Franny said.

"Don't worry," her mother said. "The boys will be awful. You'll think you're dancing with a cutting board."

They danced from one end of the living room to the other and through the dining room where poor Zeke sat next to Dr. Henry Hall, trying to finish his dinner so he could belong to the Clean Plate Club.

"I don't *want* to belong to the Clean Plate Club," Zeke was saying as his sister danced with his mother around the dining room table.

Dancing out of the room and into the kitchen,

Margaret whispered in Franny's ear, "You're getting so good, darling."

"Am I really?"

"So much better."

As she danced, smelling the sweet gardenia toilet water Margaret Hall always wore, Franny felt a kind of sizzle in her belly, imagining Mikey Houston with his greased blond bangs and blue eyes and double dimples on his cheeks, floating around the gymnasium with her.

It was also possible, she thought with a mixture of hope and fear, that no one would ask her to dance, that she'd sit at a table around the dance floor, her silver shoes hidden by her dress, watching the dancers rock back and forth on the gymnasium floor, checking the clock over the basketball net, counting the hours until the dance was over.

If she got any more nervous, it was possible that she'd throw up right on the dance floor.

Mikey Houston was by the refreshment table drinking ginger ale punch when Franny walked into the gymnasium, her left foot locked into the silver shoe in a bed of toilet paper, loosely fitted around her foot. The dance was in full swing, the dance floor crowded with jitterbugging couples flying from one another's arms, girls screaming on the sidelines, boys smoking just outside the gymnasium door, Johnny and the Teddy Bears shouting above the conversations.

Franny sat on a folding chair with Boots and Eleanor, her lap full of sugar cookies.

They were talking about boys.

"Do you see Bobby Mason with Belinda?" Eleanor said. "I hear she's really *fast*."

"I heard that too," Boots said. "My sister told me Belinda was making out with Bobby something terrible in the cemetery last Friday night."

"Behind the Freys' gravestone," Eleanor said. "You know the one that says Frey in curvy letters with the whole family, all six of them including the grandmother dying in a fire in 1925 and getting buried in the same grave."

"Icky," Franny said.

From time to time, Bobby looked over at the group of girls, a wicked half smile on his face. Franny assumed it was Eleanor that he was planning to dance with, and who wouldn't want to dance with Eleanor, she thought, a little round pumpkin of a pretty girl with melon breasts.

"Bobby's looking at *you*, Franny," Boots said.

"He *is*, Franny," Eleanor said. "He keeps looking at you out of the corner of his eye."

"He's the coolest in the ninth grade, whatever he did behind the Freys' gravestone," Boots said. "But I'd be terrified to dance with him."

"Afraid you'd be *defiled*?" Franny giggled.

"My mom says he's the kind of boy who puts his hand straight down the front of a girl's dress. That she's heard it from the other mothers at coffee after Mass at St. Bernadette's."

"I don't think he's even cute," Eleanor said. "Too greasy and pimply for me. Have you seen him close-up?"

"I like him close-up," Boots said. "He's sort of got this look and you know he carries cigarettes in his back pocket."

"The one I like is Mikey Houston," Eleanor said wistfully. "But I think he likes someone else."

"Who?" Franny asked so quickly she surprised herself.

She had been scanning the dance floor for Mikey, watching the gym door, which was open so the boys at Easterbrook could have a smoke on the blacktop, to see if Mikey was among them.

"Maybe Linda Farmer."

"I don't think Linda Farmer is his type," Franny said.

"How do you know his type?" Eleanor asked. "I didn't even know you'd ever spoken to Mikey Houston."

"I haven't." Franny shrugged. "But sometimes you just get a sense of a person." She had never told Eleanor or anyone else, including her mother, that she thought about Mikey Houston a lot, that she watched him in the halls when he wasn't looking, rode by his house on her bicycle hoping to see him playing basketball in his driveway, called him on the telephone, hanging up when he answered.

"Do you like him too?" Eleanor asked.

"I don't even know him."

"You know him as well as we do," Boots said.

"You always keep everything a secret, Franny," Eleanor said. "I never know what you think about anyone and you're my first cousin and almost best friend."

Mikey Houston was a tall and quiet, confident boy and well-liked — not like the other boys at Easterbrook High School, the athletes, the regular half-bad boys who hung out at the Sweet Shoppe, or the losers. He had deep blue eyes and when he looked at someone — and he had made eye contact with Franny Hall three times since school opened, once in the cafeteria line when they were standing side by side — he had a habit of looking directly at a person. His eyes were electric beams that seemed to see right through to the heart. Franny liked that about him especially.

In her daydreams she loved him deeply. The only conversation they had was that same day in the cafeteria line. He asked her did she have a dollar since he had left his money at home.

"Maybe only fifty cents," he'd said softly.

Franny could only shake her head, too nervous to speak.

No, I didn't bring any money to school today, she should have said. *But I will tomorrow just in case.*

Or, *I'm out of money now but maybe after school, we could meet at the Sweet Shoppe for a soda.*

Or, *I have a dollar for lunch today and I'll split lunch with you.*

Which was true since she did have a dollar for a tuna fish sandwich and a carton of milk.

Franny was just about to get another cup of lemonade when someone tapped her on the shoulder. She could feel his breath warm on the top of her head and his voice in her ear.

"Want to dance?" he asked. "Or not."

No thank you was what she should have said and beat it out of the gymnasium. She should have called Zeke, who would have been watching something like *Hopalong Cassidy* on the TV in the kitchen and asked him to tell their mother she was feeling sick.

"I *will* dance, yes," Franny said, turning to face him, almost cheek to cheek.

It was Kirk Salt leaning over her.

Behind her, she could hear Boots saying something to Eleanor, but Kirk had her by the hand, his hand sweaty even in February, and she wiggled her left foot in the toilet paper bed trying to balance and followed him to the middle of the dance floor.

Johnny and the Teddy Bears were playing a slow dance.

She knew Kirk Salt from English and math classes even though he lived in the country outside of Easterbrook. Kirk was nice and smart and boring, like a lot of the very small group of smart boys at Easterbrook, just the kind of boy willing to try his luck with Franny Hall, who was pretty enough to dance with but not exactly a catch. He wasn't the kind of boy Franny would ever day-dream about kissing, but at least if she did tip over in her silver shoes or something else dreadful happened, she'd rather be dancing with Kirk Salt than Mikey Houston.

He was so tall that her head came up to the middle of his chest. In order to talk to him she had to bend her neck way backward, her shoulders arched, his hot, putrid breath floating down on her. Johnny was singing "Tennessee Waltz," and she wondered how long it would be before the song was over.

"So," he began, struggling to think of something to say. "I guess you're trying out for cheerleader."

"No," she said so quickly that she had to come up with a reason since every girl in the ninth grade tried out for cheerleader. "I have too many other things to do so I can't." And then, not wishing to leave him with the impression that she wasn't good enough for cheerleading, she added, "Maybe sophomore year."

Cheerleading was the one predictable requirement for popularity at Easterbrook High, and Franny had thought about it, thought how it would look from the bleachers on the football field for a girl like her with lumpy shoes and a big lift and a bad limp to be a cheerleader in a little red skirt and thick sweater with a big red *E* in the middle.

"Don't try out," her father had said to her and Franny knew that he was protecting her from disappointment. "It's not a smart idea."

Sometimes she wished for another father who wasn't so careful. A father more like her mother who said, "What's to lose? You either make the squad or not."

Kirk bent down, a crooked smile on his face and asked if she wanted to go to the movies next week. Maybe her parents would let her go to the late night show. She was about to say "I can't," since she certainly didn't want to sit in a dark movie theater with Kirk Salt breathing his hot bad breath into the air next to her, when someone tapped her on the back and it was Mikey Houston.

"Can I cut in?" Mikey Houston asked, angling between Franny and Kirk Salt.

"Is it okay?" Franny asked, her heart pounding in her chest, anxious because it was Mikey Houston, not wishing to hurt Kirk Salt's feelings.

"Sure," Kirk said almost as if he were grateful and he lumbered across the floor to the refreshment table.

Mikey slipped Franny's right hand loosely in the V between his thumb and index finger. He took hold of her back just in the center and pulled her toward him with such confidence it took her breath away.

"You're Franny Hall," he said. "I've been watching you around school."

"Me too," Franny said. "I've been watching you too."

Their heads were almost together and her face close enough to feel the warmth of his breath, to notice that his dimples didn't match — one and a half dimples in the right corner of his mouth and a tiny one in the left — and that his eyes which looked blue were actually gray, although the lights had been dimmed in the gymnasium.

"You're noticeable," he said.

She was sure that he had taken note of her because of her problem, that he'd watched from behind as she limped down the second-floor corridor of Easterbrook High.

"Because of the way I walk?" she asked, and her voice, even in her own ears, sounded casual.

"No," he said. "You have a cute way of walking but you're noticeable because your hair's so black you look foreign."

"My mother's Danish."

"No, I mean really foreign. Like from India."

"So is that good?"

"It's good to me. Nobody I know in Easterbrook has such black hair."

Mikey rested his chin on the top of her head, just that much taller than she was, only a head, and Franny thought she was going to explode.

The music was picking up and he pulled back, turning his head from side to side in time to the rhythm, still holding hard on to Franny's hand, his other hand firmly on her back and she was keeping up with him at that pace. But if the music got any faster, she knew she'd have to sit out the dance.

Maybe he didn't care about her clunky shoes or the way she tilted side to side when she walked. Maybe he thought she was pretty.

"Here they go," he said as the tempo of Johnny and the Teddy Bears got faster and faster, but as Mikey swung her away from him into all the other jitterbugging couples, Franny lost the rhythm.

Boots dancing with Bilbo Nutley accidentally stepped on the toe of her silver shoes and Franny, tipping to the left, felt herself losing control.

"Too fast?" Mikey asked.

She nodded.

And almost as if the band were listening, the music slowed down, Mikey pulled her close, her head tucked barely under his chin, and he was more or less rocking back and forth in the middle of the room. She was grateful for the slow sway of swing music since her foot pressed up against the hard knot of toilet paper hurt, and it felt to her as if the cushion of paper had disappeared.

She closed her eyes and lay her cheek against the nubby roughness of his wool jacket.

At first, she didn't notice that people had stopped dancing and were looking in her direction, looking at the floor, looking at her.

She stopped still.

"Franny," Boots said in a stage whisper. "Look behind you."

She dropped Mikey Houston's hand and turned around.

Behind her, streaming in a long ribbon of white from under the black velvet skirt of her dress, was the toilet paper her mother so carefully had laced around her foot, stuffed into the toe of her silver shoe.

The president of the student council was standing on the stage with the microphone ready to announce the king and queen of the Valentine's Dance but Franny was limping toward the girls' room as fast as she could, across the dance floor, weaving in and out among the dancers.

Mikey Houston was standing where she had left him in the middle of the dance floor with a group of boys. She saw him when she turned to go into the bathroom.

There were four cubicles and she went into the last one, closed the door behind her, locked it, sat on the toilet seat, and pulled her feet up so no one coming into the girls' room would know she was there.

She would wait until the dance was over. Until the last person had left the gymnasium and her worried father was the only parent left standing outside in the freezing cold.

Franny took off the silver shoes, dropped the remaining toilet paper into the toilet, stood on the toilet seat, and tossed the shoes in the trash can by the sink, waiting for the music to stop, for the dance to be over, for the gymnasium to empty out of people.

ISOLATION WARD

Franny sat on her unmade bed painting her fingernails with the cherry red polish that she got in her stocking from Saint Nicholas. It was Sunday. Until that morning, she had never had a desire to paint her ragged nails, which were ugly from years of nervous biting. Now, sitting on her bed the morning after the Valentine's Dance, the door to her room locked, she decided cherry red would improve the nasty little stubs of nail. It made her feel better to be doing something, anything at all to keep from thinking about the dance.

She had locked herself in her bedroom for the rest of her life. That was her plan when she woke up in darkness in the middle of the night and couldn't fall back to sleep, grateful when the darkness paled and she could hear her family getting ready for the day.

The house was old and drafty and thin walled, so it was easy to overhear her mother on the telephone with Aunt Estelle before the sun came up. Her father and mother had an argument outside her bedroom and Franny had heard her father say, "You've got to stop trying so hard with Franny. She'll do what she does in her own time."

Zeke sat outside her bedroom door knocking every few minutes.

"Fraaaaanny," he'd call. "Please open the door."

But she didn't answer.

"I know you're in there," he said, his mouth around the keyhole or under the door where there was a space.

Franny had no intention of speaking to any of her family. She held every one of them responsible for her humiliation because they were related to her by blood and lived in the house with her and were supposed to understand her better than anyone else in the world.

But mainly she blamed her mother.

In her English notebook, she wrote a note to Zeke.

Dear Ezekiel,

Please tell your mother that I threw the silver shoes into the trash can in the girls' room beside the gymnasium in case she wants to find them and get her money back from Eldridges.

Franny

She slipped the note under the door and Zeke must have snatched it.

"Mamaaaaa," he called, slapping barefoot down the steps. "We got a letter from Franny!"

She didn't have a plan, although she doubted she would be going to school for a long time. She would refuse to talk to Boots or to Eleanor who had been witnesses to what had happened at the dance. She hoped never to see Kirk Salt again and if she caught sight of Mikey Houston, most likely she would die.

But she was perfectly happy in her room. It was almost pleasant to imagine remaining there for weeks. Everything she needed was there, including her own bathroom and twelve windows on three sides of the room from which to watch the town of Easterbrook.

The walls were painted pale blue, her bedspread white, and there was a small chair, a *reading chair* her mother called it, covered in blue and white stripes, a desk that had belonged to her grandmother Hall, and a dresser that had belonged to her great-aunt Florence, and photographs of all of her Danish relatives including her dead grandmother, the mother her own mother never knew. The blue and white was cool in summer and bright in winter against the steady gray blanketing the landscape outside her windows.

She was getting hungry.

Hunger was going to present a problem, she was thinking, when Zeke called, "Franny! Boots is here with Eleanor."

Franny leaned back in her bed and closed her eyes, listening to the annoying *click, click, click* of her mother's high-heeled shoes on the hardwood floor stairs.

"Darling," Margaret Hall called from the other side of the door, which Franny had locked. "Boots and Eleanor are here to see you."

Franny didn't open her eyes, listening to hear if Boots or Eleanor would tell what had happened at the dance the night before.

"Could you come out and talk to them?" her mother asked.

"Franny isn't going to talk to them," Zeke said. "I promise."

"Should I tell them to leave, Franny?"

And after a few long moments of silence, Margaret Hall spoke again, more quietly.

"I will tell them to come back another time," she said,

and Franny listened for her high heels on the wooden stairs.

"Would you like toast and jam, Franny?" Zeke whispered through the door when they had left.

Franny very much wanted toast and jam, actually toast slathered in butter with a little raspberry jam from the berries her mother had put up in the fall.

"I would."

"I'll get it for you," Zeke said. "I'll make the toast all by myself in the toaster. Two pieces. Do you want ice cream?"

"No thank you, Ezekiel. Just toast."

Minutes later, Zeke was back knocking on the door.

"The toast is ready," he said.

"Leave it outside. I'm not going to open the door until you're downstairs, Zeke. Until I hear your feet on the wood steps."

"How come?"

"I don't want anyone to see me at all."

"How do you look?"

"It doesn't matter. I look how I look and don't want anyone to see that. You understand?"

"No."

"I don't want you to see me ever again."

"In my life?"

"That's right but we can talk between the doors. We can talk whenever you want. Okay?"

"No." And his voice was full of tears. "It's not okay."

On Monday morning, the second day after the dance, Franny was up early before the sun, writing a letter to Zeke. It was her thirteenth letter to Zeke since Sunday morning, most of them short.

Dear Ezekiel,

I'd like a bologna sandwich for lunch and a Coke and a dill pickle.

Your former sister, Francine, 10 a.m. Feb. 12

Or

Dear Ezekiel,

Would you please let your mother, Margaret Hall, know that whenever she talks to her sister, Estelle, on the telephone, I can hear every word she says. Every stupid word she says.

Your former sister, Francine, 2 p.m. Feb. 12

Or

Dear Ezekiel,

I don't want lamb patties and creamed spinach for dinner. I'd like a bowl of chocolate ice cream and another dill pickle.

Your former sister, Francine, 6:30 p.m. Feb. 12

Or the last letter before she turned out her light on Sunday night.

Dear Ezekiel,

Thank you for your help and I know you can't read very well, but I assume that someone in the Hall household is still capable of reading the English language and your job with these letters is simply to be a messenger. Give them to Dr. Henry Hall or Margaret Hall.

Sincerely yours, F., 9:30 p.m. Feb. 12

Franny's mother knocked on the door to her bedroom at six-thirty in the morning on Monday. Already Franny was wide awake writing a letter to Zeke.

"Darling? Six-thirty. Time to get up for school."

Franny leaned back against the pillow. She couldn't

believe that her mother actually thought that she had any intention of going to school.

Was Margaret Hall simply following Dr. Henry Hall's recommendation that *the best defense is a good offense*? Was she actually thinking that Franny believed her cheerful voice pretending *everything is just fine, normal as usual, we're happy as clams at the Hall house located smack in the middle of Easterbrook, Ohio*?

Was her mother crazy?

Dear Ezekiel,

What you need to understand now at six years old is that YOU should be the judge of your own actions. You may not understand that now but you better get started. I COMPLETELY trusted Margaret Hall, formerly my mother, to have my best interest in mind when she dressed me up like a clown to go to the Valentine's Dance at Easterbrook High. And I was wrong.

I'm telling you this because it's Monday morning and I am NOT going to school but I AM thinking that I owe it to you as your former sister to warn you against my former parents, particularly Margaret.

Please remind your parents about my decision regarding school and ask that they take care of their own problems and leave mine to me.

Thank you. YFS (meaning Your Former Sister), Francine

Just after her mother knocked on her door, about the same time her father usually left for the hospital unless there was an emergency, Franny could hear Dr. Hall stomping up the steps to the second floor. Other families had carpet on their steps, wall-to-wall carpet in every room but the kitchen, usually the same color for every room. For instance Eleanor's parents, who were after all related to Franny, had a Williamsburg blue carpet even in the bathrooms, and Boots's family, who didn't really have enough money for wall-to-wall carpet, had thin brown carpet everywhere in the house except the kitchen.

"Daddy's coming upstairs to talk to you," Zeke announced through the keyhole.

Franny didn't respond, waiting with only the slightest anxiety for her former father to *bang, bang, bang* on her door as he was inclined to do when he was angry.

Which he did. *Bang, bang, bang*, followed by "FRANCINE."

"She won't talk, Daddy," Zeke said. "I promise."

"She's going to talk to me if I have to break the door down."

Franny stood up to check how she looked in the mirror just in case her father *was* able to break down the door. Her hair was tangled, her face a little pale, but otherwise she looked exactly the way she had always looked. Which surprised her because she was a changed girl since the Valentine's Dance on Saturday night. Even her blood seemed to be flowing faster and warmer and in another direction.

"FRANCINE." *Bang, bang, bang.*

Downstairs, Franny could clearly hear her mother's high heels skittering across the floor from the kitchen to the hall, up the steps, and stopping outside her door.

"Please, Henry."

"She's going to school, Margaret. She's a perfectly healthy fourteen-year-old girl in a bad humor and a bad humor is not sufficient reason to skip school."

"She's had a sadness, Henry."

"A what? A sadness? Pull yourself together, Margaret. Sadness is not, according to my medical books, a terminal illness."

Franny pulled her knees up under her chin, wrapped her arms around her legs, and listened with a certain pleasure, a certain inescapable satisfaction not equal to the embarrassment of the Valentine's Dance but at least some compensation for the helplessness she had felt.

Zeke screamed "STOP." Margaret Hall *clicked, clicked* down the steps and Dr. Henry Hall said nothing.

But Franny heard the car start underneath her window and supposed that he was off to work, turning on the radio to the classical music station, considering his only daughter's failure as an agreeable girl, no longer *good as gold*.

Later, Franny, still locked in her bedroom, started the first murder mystery story of what might be her writing career, *The Terror of the Missing Silver Shoes*, which began with her father's statement:

"According to the medical books, sadness is not a terminal illness."

On Tuesday and Wednesday, it snowed, a little sun filtering through the snow clouds, and Franny stretched out on the comforter, thinking.

Her life in her bedroom was simple. Every morning she got up, took a shower, dressed in jeans and her pajama top, opened her bedroom door just long enough to get the breakfast which had been left on a tray on the floor, and sat down at her desk to write.

The Terror of the Missing Silver Shoes kept her from thinking about Mikey Houston and the toilet paper streaming along the gymnasium floor, about her mother's betrayal, about the future of her life in Easterbrook, Ohio.

But days in her bedroom began to seem long.

She had started writing philosophical notes to Zeke since the practical matters, primarily food, had been taken care of and three meals a day were delivered on time, along with snacks and an occasional missive from her mother.

Dear Ezekiel,

I wish we were closer to the same age. Eight years is a long time now. When I am twenty and free to move to China where I plan to go work with Chinese orphans, you will only be twelve and in the eighth grade and I'll be an adult. I could get married at eighteen. Certainly after China, I'll go to college. But by the time you're twenty-one and I'm twenty-nine, we'll be more or less the same age and we will be able to talk at the same level of understanding.

Now I feel a responsibility to protect you from things your father and mother failed to protect you from. Toughness is important. The other day when Ernie

Sang beat you up in the Sangs' backyard, your mother flew over and swooped you up and said some unpleasant things to Mrs. Sang and brought you home for a chocolate sundae. Most children have to fend for themselves. That's what I mean by toughness. Your parents are overprotective.

Sometimes I think it's a good thing that I'm crippled. I've known bad things since I was born, most especially that people can be very unkind and you have to ignore it.

That's all for now. YFS, Francine

It was about ten in the morning and Zeke was at school, Dr. Henry Hall at the hospital, and Margaret in her study drawing the curly noodles of an elephant's brain for a new book on elephants from Chicago University Press. The house was quiet, Franny was sleepy and bored, the book she was planning to write had not started to unravel in her imagination.

She heard the door to her mother's study open and the click of her high heels.

A manila envelope was slipped under her bedroom door.

"Franny, are you there?" she asked in her cheery voice. "I have something for you."

"No, I'm not here," Franny said.

"Well, when you come back, I've put an article you might enjoy under your door."

Franny smiled in spite of herself.

Margaret Hall had stopped asking questions about the dance and inquiring after Franny's state of mind, had stopped asking her to call Boots and Eleanor and some other girls in her class who kept calling asking after her. Now she only asked simple questions, with simple answers, no complications.

Sometimes Franny was urgent to talk to her mother, to tell her about the mystery she was writing, to report the story of what had really happened at the Valentine's Dance, to tell her that Mikey Houston had actually asked *her* to dance and then the toilet paper thing happened and she fled to the girls' room, locking herself in a cubicle. But those moments of longing for her mother's conversation were fleeting, overcome by the small hot ball of fury Franny was still nursing.

SALVATORE FERRAGAMO: SHOEMAKER TO THE STARS

The story — clipped from the February issue of *Vogue* magazine, Margaret Hall's very favorite fashion magazine, which she read every month cover to cover — was a color photographic essay with some text. Salvatore Ferragamo, a small, delicate Italian man, was pictured in his shoe factory outside of Florence. In another photograph he was with his wife and grown children in the showroom in Florence, kneeling among his shoes, holding one scarlet and black high-heeled shoe up for a tall, bony, flat-chested blonde to examine. There were all kinds of shoes, beautiful shoes with high heels and even higher heels in every color, every material. And beautiful women, actresses and artists, countesses and wealthy Americans, trying on Salvatore Ferragamo's shoes, admiring reflections of their feet and legs in the low gilt-framed mirrors, in the full-size mirrors. In the final picture, Salvatore Ferragamo stood in the center with a young woman, her arm laced through his.

FERRAGAMO WITH HIS BELOVED DAUGHTER, FLAVIA.

Franny folded the article and put it on her desk, starting another letter to Zeke who would be coming home from school soon, a Thursday, dismissal at two. It was almost two and snowing again in long white sheets outside her window.

Dear Ezekiel, she wrote. I don't know what is going on with your mother, something to worry about certainly, but NOW she has pushed an article about a shoemaker under my door as if I would have an interest in shoemakers. I wonder if I could trouble you to tell her to Stop the Shoe Pressure. SSP. Stop the Shoe Pressure. I have all the shoes I need. Tell her that. Two pairs, one black leather and one brown leather, high-tops, laces, heavy lift on the left shoe. That's ME. Francine, Your Former Sister

"Frannnnnnnny." Zeke galloped up the stairs, stopping just short of Franny's bedroom. "Are you still there?"

Franny got up, dropped the Ferragamo article in the drawer of her desk where she kept the chewing gum she wasn't allowed to chew in public, and pushed the letter to Zeke under her door.

"Guess what," Zeke called. "Guess what, Franny?"

She opened her desk drawer, took out a stick of Wrigley's Spearmint, and popped it in her mouth.

"I don't know, Ezekiel. What? I guess you better tell me."

"I saw Mikey Houston picking up his little brother at school and he asked where you were and were you sick because you'd disappeared right in the middle of dancing with him and so I said you were under the weather. That's what Mama is telling people. *Franny is actually under the weather* is what she says."

Franny took out another piece of paper, writing:

I'm not under the weather. I'm in a bad humor. You can tell people that. F.

She folded the paper, wrote *Margaret Hall*, and slipped the note under her bedroom door.

Her heart was beating in her mouth with the news that Mikey Houston had inquired about her. She flopped on her back on the bed, a little giddy, and closed her eyes.

She believed her little brother. Why would a six-year-old boy like Ezekiel Hall make up something like that? But it was also possible that Mikey H. had been laughing with his friends all week about the train of toilet paper following Franny to the girls' room, laughing about her lumpy feet. He probably was glad to have some interesting news to tell the boys in the ninth grade so he could say, "Guys, wanna know about Franny Hall?" and they'd say, "Yeah!" laughing along, and Mikey Houston would say, "Well I have it straight from her brother Ezekiel that Franny's under the weather!" and they'd laugh themselves silly, slapping their thighs, making *cripple* jokes one after the other.

Franny turned off the light beside her bed and climbed under the covers. It was early evening and dark, dark enough to go to bed, to fall asleep, to put this day with its growing sadness behind her. But she was a stubborn girl, born stubborn with a strong will, and had no intention of changing her plans, only of falling asleep so Thursday would be over and she could have tomorrow when she woke up.

In the distance, she listened to the house noises like background music — her mother talking to Eleanor and then to Boots — *under the weather* Margaret Hall said again and again, to Mr. Hoagland, the principal, to her sister-in-law Gabbie, who was Eleanor's mother, to Estelle although Estelle already knew the real story, even to Dr. Henry Hall when he called from the hospital to see if there had been any change. Franny was, as she had heard him say to his wife, *a difficult child recently given to moods.*

Dr. Hall had an emergency call around nine o'clock. He called to Margaret, already upstairs reading with Zeke, that he was off to the emergency room and it could be a long night.

In the bedroom next to hers, Zeke was begging his mother not to turn off the light, to stay with him, that he was afraid.

"Why are you afraid, Zekey?" Margaret Hall asked.

"Everything is different."

"Everything is the same, darling."

"It's not the same," Zeke said. "Franny won't come out of her room and she told me I might never get to see her again."

Margaret must have whispered some sweetness to Zeke because he stopped talking and then Franny heard her mother's high heels travel across the hardwood floor and down the corridor to her own room.

She turned over on her side and squished her pillow around her face, burrowing in it.

Poor Zeke. Perhaps she ought to tell him that of course they would see each other again. She didn't know when that would be. But not forever.

It pleased her to know that she was so important to Zeke that he was afraid to go to sleep at night. She needed to write him a reassuring letter to let him know that in spite of the failure of their parents, he was still her brother — a *Dear Ezekiel, You are the best brother in Easterbrook* kind of letter.

Franny had almost fallen asleep, the light still on beside her bed, her writing notebook on her stomach, when she heard her former mother's footsteps again and the rustle of paper underneath her door. She waited until Margaret had gone back to her own bedroom, then she opened the door so her cat, Pickle, could sleep on the foot of her bed, and closed it, tiptoeing across the floor with the piece of paper her mother had pushed under the door.

Dear Francine, the letter began.
I HAVE A PLAN.
Yr. former mother, Margaret Hall

Two

A DIFFERENT TOMORROW

Franny left her room for the first time eight days after the Valentine's Dance. It was a Monday morning, early, just after her father had driven Zeke to school on his way to the hospital and her mother had left for the Cleveland airport to pick up Aunt Estelle, who would be spending the last week of February with them.

Franny was alone in the house. She walked barefoot in her pajamas through the rooms, carrying a discontented Pickle under her arm, checking her parents' bedroom, her mother's office, her father's study piled with books and papers, pictures that he'd never got around to hanging of his children, his wife, his brother as a boy, all leaning against the wall, Zeke's bedroom, the bed crowded with stuffed animals. Nothing had changed since she had gone into retreat. The house even smelled of toast and coffee as it had every morning of her life.

She had gone to bed the night before as usual with a hot ball of temper like fever in her head and awakened feeling actually well, as if she were recovering from a bad case of the flu. During the night while she was sleeping, the sickness had lifted and her body turned a corner on its way to health.

As usual, Margaret Hall had left breakfast on a tray outside her room, which Franny took downstairs and ate at the table in the kitchen. On the tray, her mother had put a note saying she'd be back with Aunt Estelle by eleven and maybe Franny would come downstairs to see her aunt. She put her dishes in the sink and dropped the note in a wastebasket.

Dear Zeke, she had written the night before. I am not looking forward to the visit of your aunt Estelle tomorrow. Please explain to her that I have divorced the Hall family, except you, of course. Forever and ever, Franny

Franny liked the sound of the word *divorce*. Leah Penelton's parents were divorced and so was Miss Jones who taught second grade, and occasionally her father expressed a wish that his older brother, Eleanor's father, would divorce Eleanor's ill-tempered mother, Gabriela.

It never occurred to her that her parents would divorce, even when they fought. Even when her father stormed out of the house or her mother said in a stage whisper to her father, *I could always return to Denmark with the children*. They were married and loved each other and that was that.

But it had occurred to her in the last week that *she* could divorce her family, simply call herself Franny or Francine, no longer a Hall, but a free-floating, unattached girl who could make such a decision without a transfusion of new blood.

When it came to family, *blood* was her father's favorite word. *Blood is thicker than water*, he would say about his own family. *We have to stick together through thick and thin*.

When Franny was younger, she wondered what he meant by thick and thin and whether blood was really thicker than water. Were these things her father knew because he was a doctor? But she never asked him because his answers would be too long and scientific and she was, besides, a little afraid of him, although her mother had insisted that she was the *apple of his eye*.

Since Franny moved into her bedroom, her parents had been fighting about her. She could hear their arguments even with the doors closed. She had never worried about her parents' marriage the way Eleanor did about her parents'. They loved each other, especially her father loved her mother and thought she was the most beautiful woman in Ohio, maybe anywhere. But they had almost never fought. If Margaret Hall was upset about something, she kept it to herself.

It pleased Franny, these arguments about her.

"Oh Henry," her mother would say. "Poor Franny is brokenhearted."

"She is *not* brokenhearted," Dr. Hall said loud enough that Franny could imagine Zeke putting a pillow over his head to shut out the sound of Dr. Hall's voice, worried tears gathering in Ezekiel's eyes.

"Franny is difficult on the way to intolerable," he said. "Stop indulging her."

"She's *good*, Henry. You've always said yourself she's *good as gold*."

"Get a grip, Margaret," her father would say with the full resonance of his large voice. "*Good* is not necessarily good for Franny. She needs to speak up for herself instead of lurking behind her bedroom door feeling sorry for herself."

"Get a grip, Franny," he said as he passed Franny's door on his way to the hospital that morning.

And he bounded down the stairs as if he were hammering each step, hoping to make the house collapse on them all.

All week, she had sat in bed at night after dinner, after Zeke was tucked in and her parents were in their own bedroom with the door ajar, and listened to them fight.

Poor darling Franny, her mother would say.

Poor darling Franny, Franny thought to herself, beginning to hate the thought of it, the sound of it, the word *poor* assigned to her name.

Over the last weekend in the solitude of her bedroom, she was beginning to feel a kind of internal metamorphosis taking place, as if she were in the process of becoming someone different from the girl she'd been in elementary school, the sweet, accommodating, agreeable girl everybody had loved and taken for granted.

Poor darling Franny was not the girl she wished to be.

The night before, very late after the argument between her parents had ended and the house was quiet, Margaret Hall had slipped a letter under the door.

Dear Signor Salvatore Ferragamo, the letter dated 22 February 1956 began:

I was pleased to read in the American magazine called Vogue about your astonishing career and have always admired the beauty of your shoes. But I was surprised and touched to discover that you came by making shoes as a result of an accident that affected your walking.

I have such a dilemma with my treasured daughter Franny, who was born with crippled feet and therefore cannot be a comfortable part of the merriment and romance that comes of being a young, young woman. She wears heavy orthopedic shoes with a high lift on one shoe and her feet are terribly, painfully crippled. It would be an honor and a privilege if you might consider making a last for Franny's feet so that she could have your beautiful shoes to go to dances without embarrassment.

I am Danish, married to an American physician and we live in a very small town in the middle of this vast country. We are certainly not wealthy like the clientele pictured with you in Vogue magazine, but I would do anything in my power for my daughter's happiness.

Yours truly, Margaret Groener Hall

Franny folded the letter and put it in the drawer with the Juicy Fruit chewing gum and Milky Way bars that Zeke had bought with his own allowance money at Grace's Variety. Then she climbed in bed and closed her eyes but couldn't sleep. At first it was the light from the top of St. James's steeple keeping her awake and then the sound of the wind cracking the frozen branches on the trees outside her window. And then streaming through her brain was the letter her mother had written to Ferragamo.

What if this shoemaker answered her mother's letter? What if he invited Franny to come to Italy? What if she went?

As a slow sleep came over her, Franny imagined herself walking into first-period math class the next morning, taking her seat in the front of the class. She would be wearing her plaid skirt, kneesocks, and a crispy white blouse, her hair in a ponytail.

"Hi, guys," she'd say as if nothing whatever had happened at the Valentine's Dance. "I probably should let you know that I'll be away in Florence, Italy, for a while."

Which had at least the possibility of being true.

Walking down College Street as the late February sun eased its ball of pale, pale light over the Ohio horizon, she felt triumphant to be leaving without her parents' knowledge, to have missed five days of school without the excuse of an illness, to be in charge of her own life.

There was nothing at all that anyone could *make* her do. Not at school and not at home.

At Scioto Street, Franny turned toward the square in the center of town, stopping at the soda shop for a double-dip chocolate ice-cream cone.

"Ice cream so early in the morning?" Mr. Litey asked, scooping a ball of chocolate into a wafer cone.

Franny pushed her quarters across the counter.

"Aren't you late for school?" he asked.

"I am," she said without explanation.

She took the cone, wrapped the wafer in a napkin, and walked the three blocks to the high school slowly so she could finish her ice cream.

She had not planned this day. She had no story formed for facing her classmates at Easterbrook. Or seeing Mikey Houston or Kirk Salt or Eleanor or Boots.

But in the days she had spent alone in her room, she had come to know that she would never again allow herself to be humiliated. Whatever it took to protect her dignity, she would do.

Boots, who was sitting at the top of the high school steps, squealed.

"Fraaaaanny!" she called. "Where have you been?"

"At home in my bedroom," Franny said, dropping down beside Boots.

"In bed?"

"Nope. Just in my bedroom. Living there," she said. "What are you doing outside in the cold during math class?"

"My mom's picking me up for a dentist appointment." She flung her arm around Franny's shoulder. "How come you never called me?"

Franny shrugged.

"I just didn't," she said, which was the truth.

"I kept trying to call you. Eleanor and I went over to your house and then your mom said you were really sick."

"I wasn't really sick," Franny said. "I was OFF school."

"OFF school?"

"I didn't want to be here."

"And now you're ON school?"

"Now I'm here by choice," Franny said. "School is not a requirement as far as I know."

"It's the law."

"Maybe in your house because you're Catholic but not in mine."

"I think it's the United States government law. I'll ask my mom."

"I think I'm right," Franny said.

"I hope so," Boots said. "I'm already sick of high school but my mom would drag me to school by my hair if I tried to stay home."

"She couldn't," Franny said. "That's the point. You're taller and stronger than she is and she couldn't drag you seventeen blocks by your hair. She'd be arrested." She finished her cone and pushed her hands in the pockets of her coat. "So what's been going on?"

"Nothing much," Boots said. "The usual. I got in trouble about the dance because I was late and my mom says that's kaput for dances."

"And that's all?"

"Well, on Tuesday Bobby Mason broke his femur jumping off the roof of our garage and my dad is pretty furious. And also Eleanor's going steady with Mikey Houston just like that. And something else which I forget."

Franny's heart stopped.

"Eleanor and Mikey Houston?"

"You didn't know?"

"I haven't talked to anyone on the phone including you," Franny said, feeling her blood heat up, her face flush pink.

"But Eleanor's your cousin!"

"I don't keep track of everything Eleanor does in her life," Franny said.

Not that she had loved Mikey Houston anyway, she told herself. He was soft and pinky-skinned with pimples bigger than his dimples, something she hadn't noticed until she danced with him. Probably his breath was skunky and she hadn't noticed that either.

But Eleanor Hall was not to be trusted — not in the way Franny trusted Boots, who would never speak behind her back to other friends or make fun of her walk or betray Franny's secrets. Eleanor would do all of those things and had even stolen her red sweater with her initials F.H. for Francine Hall and stuffed it between her mattress and box springs. Not that Franny told anyone about the sweater or even confronted Eleanor. She didn't want to lose her cousin's friendship, counting on her father's belief that *blood is thicker than water*.

But maybe *blood* didn't matter to Eleanor, who at the moment was burning to crispy toast in Franny's ferocious mind.

"I'll see you later," Franny called when Boots's mother drove into the school parking lot. She pulled open the heavy door of the high school building, dropped her coat on the floor of her locker, and headed to math class.

Eleanor was sitting in the back, pink-cheeked from winter cold, her curly hair piled up on the top of her head with a saucy green bow, her round kitten face scrunched up in a smile.

"Hi, Franny, Franny, Franny," she said in a stage whisper.

Franny walked to the front of the class and took her seat next to AJ Waters. In the next desk, Mikey Houston was drawing a cartoon on a page of algebra problems.

"Hello, Franny." Mr. Eckard, the algebra teacher, spoke as if he were making an announcement so everyone could hear. "How very nice to have you back with us. Are you feeling better?"

"I wasn't sick." Franny reached in her bag and took out a pencil and notebook. "I was absent."

"You were absent for a week as I've made note of in my grade book and I had word from your mother that you were sick."

"I wasn't *exactly* sick," she said, tearing a piece of lined paper out of her notebook.

Dear Mikey, she wrote. Sorry I left you abruptly on the dance floor. I had to leave in a hurry as you probably know. Yours sincerely, Franny

She handed the note to AJ to pass to Mikey who wrote on the back of it, handing the paper back to AJ.

"Well," Mr. Eckard replied, turning to write formulas on the blackboard. "Maybe your mother *thought* you were sick."

Hi, Franny. Your mom told the school that you were under the weather. Did you get sick at the dance? Mikey

You know what happened to me at the dance, Franny wrote back. I wasn't under the weather. I didn't want to come to school and so I didn't. Franny

At least she should say something true.

"Cool!" Mikey said when the bell for the end of class rang. "So your mom just let you stay at home?"

"More or less," Franny said. "She couldn't exactly make me go to school."

"Let's trade moms," he said, heading out the door.

"What did your mom mean by *under the weather*?" Eleanor asked after class, catching up with Franny who was walking down the corridor to chorus. "She told my mom that you had appendicitis."

"Well, it wasn't appendicitis," Franny said, wondering what her mother had really said. It was typical of Margaret Hall to be polite and careful and keep things to herself.

"My mom says there was nothing wrong with you and it was probably because of the toilet paper coming out of your shoe like it did that made you stay at home."

Franny pushed through the door to the girls' room, Eleanor following her to the next cubicle, talking over the wall between them.

"I mean *I* would have been humiliated," Eleanor said.

"Your mother is incorrect about the toilet paper," Franny said. "I was annoyed, not humiliated."

"So I guess you heard about Mikey Houston." Eleanor adjusted the green bow in her hair in the mirror over the sink.

"I heard you're going steady."

"I mean we have sodas together at the soda shop most every afternoon."

"Nice."

"You don't mind, do you?"

Eleanor followed Franny through the door to the music room, crossing in front of the piano just as Miss Bloom was playing "Somewhere Over the Rainbow."

"Mind what?"

"Mind that I'm with Mikey since he was the one you were dancing with and who knows?"

"I'm not in love with Mikey Houston if that's what you're asking."

She climbed the steps of the small auditorium.

"He has pimples, the oozy kind," she said.

"Franny Hall." Miss Bloom stopped playing as Franny sat down next to Pixie Cooper, blonde, blue-eyed, perfect Pixie, the size of a small doll.

"We *missed* you," Miss Bloom went on. "I'm hoping you'll do a solo for the March concert."

"I may be away," Franny said.

"You can't be away," Miss Bloom said, moving her tiny little hands like a fan. "Where will you be? Everyone in town comes to the spring concert."

"I may have to be in Florence," Franny said.

"Ohio?" Miss Bloom sat down on the piano bench. "My aunt Ruby lives in Florence, Ohio."

"Florence, Italy," Franny said with a sudden rush of feeling.

Just to say *I may have to be in Florence* transformed the moment to possibility. Not that she *would* be there but that she could be. She could go to Florence and leave them all behind in the little town of Easterbrook, *an ink dot on the map of Ohio*, as her father would say.

Everyone in chorus turned around to look at Franny. *Florence, Italy*, they said, astonished as if it were as remote from Easterbrook as the planet Saturn or the moon.

"I am not happy about this, Franny," Miss Bloom said in her little voice. "I was counting on you to sing with Kirk Salt and Sally Ann Fergusen. I've set up the program and am depending on you to sing 'Somewhere Over the Rainbow' just like Judy Garland. Yours will be the only solo." She shook her head, playing a chord on the piano for silence. "Okay, everyone . . ."

And she played the opening of "America the Beautiful."

"One, two, three . . ." Miss Bloom called out.

"You upset her," AJ whispered in Franny's ear.

"How do you go to Italy?" Pixie asked.

"On a boat from New York."

"How come you're going?" Pixie asked.

"For fun," Franny said as if it were perfectly normal to go to Florence, Italy, in the middle of the school year, to leave Easterbrook, Ohio, where nearly everyone who lived there, like Franny, had been born there and stayed until they died.

"What about school?" Pixie asked.

"I'll just miss school," Franny said.

She leaned back on the bench. Eleanor, sitting in the next row, was whispering to Belinda Rae. Kirk Salt came in late.

"Honest to God, you're allowed to miss school to go to Italy?" Pixie asked.

"It's sort of a business trip," Franny said, a certain lightness flooding her body. "It hasn't happened yet but I may be invited to go."

"Ready," Miss Bloom said, her small hands perched over the piano keys like so many birds. *"O beautiful for spacious skies / For amber waves of grain / For purple mountain majesties / Above the fruited plain! / America! America! / God shed His grace on thee / And crown thy good with brotherhood / From sea to shining sea!"*

"What's going on with you?" Eleanor asked, following her cousin down the steps after the final bell at three o'clock. "Why did you say that about Mikey? It's like you went to bed sweet and woke up in the morning mean."

"Maybe you just don't know me very well."

"Of course I know you. We're cousins!"

At South Street, Franny headed toward home.

"I thought you were coming to the soda shop with me?" Eleanor said.

"My aunt Estelle is here," Franny said. "I can't."

Mean was good, Franny thought, walking up the steps to her house.

Don't let friends like Eleanor walk all over you, her mother had said to her just a few weeks ago.

Margaret Hall kept notes for self-improvement stuck in the mirror over her dressing table. *No cookies*, she'd write. *Read one book a week. Say NO to Henry at least once a day.* And a big red circle with the new message *Don't buy more shoes.*

Walking up the front steps to her porch, Franny thought of two notes to stick on her own bulletin board:

No presents for friendship.

Say what you think.

Estelle was sitting at the kitchen table drinking coffee, her feet up on one of the chairs while Margaret made tea. They were speaking Danish. Franny loved it when they spoke Danish together although she didn't understand what was said. But the strange and guttural sound of Danish in Easterbrook made her feel exotic by association.

"Hello, darling," her mother said, making no mention of the fact that Franny was out of her bedroom and had gone to school, acting as if nothing whatever had happened in the last week, as though it was perfectly normal to see Franny come in the back door and kiss her aunt Estelle. "How was school?"

"Great," Franny said, sitting across from Estelle wondering how it could be that her aunt was related by blood to Margaret Hall. She was dumpy and blonde with a reddish face almost exactly square and green eyes and no style whatsoever. It was as if she'd just arrived in her work clothes to clean the house.

"I thought you were spending the year in your room," Estelle said. "A pity, I'd thought, a waste of opportunity. And here you are!"

"I had a good time in my room," Franny said casually.

"What did you do all day?" Estelle asked, taking a sand cookie, passing the plate to Franny.

"I started to write a mystery called *The Terror of the Missing Silver Shoes*. It's autobiographical except for a murder."

Estelle shrugged.

"I like murder," she said, "but I don't like mysteries so don't count on me to read it."

Margaret put a teapot on the table and poured Franny a glass of milk.

"Estelle and I were just talking about my letter to Signor Ferragamo, the one you read this morning," Margaret said, changing the subject.

"Totally nuts for your mother to think that Signor Ferragamo is going to make shoes for you, but it's a cute idea and a good letter."

"An okay letter," Franny said.

"Margaret hasn't even thought how you'll get to Italy in the middle of the winter or how much it will cost. A fortune, I assume," Estelle said. "Does Henry have a fortune, Margaret?"

"We're actually pretty poor," Franny said, slipping out of her boots, tucking her feet under her. "In the letter Margaret wrote to Signor Ferragamo, she says that we're short on money."

"I said *not wealthy*," Margaret said. "I didn't say poor."

"I was telling your mother that I doubted Signor Ferragamo reads English."

"Maybe he doesn't read English, Estelle," Margaret said. "But he did live in Hollywood for a long time before he moved back to Italy and they speak English in Hollywood."

She slipped a cigarette out of the pack and pushed it across the table for her sister.

"I was hoping you'd know of a translator from English to Italian in New York so at least we can send Ferragamo the letter in Italian."

"Perhaps I can find someone," Estelle said, lighting the cigarette. "I actually know an Italian professor who teaches at Columbia University."

"Perfect," Margaret said. "I want to give us every chance."

"I may not be able to go to Italy," Franny said. "I've been asked to sing a solo in the spring concert."

"You may not be *invited* to go to Italy, so it doesn't matter what you may or may not do when you have nothing to decide," Estelle said.

"We can go after spring vacation if you've got a solo, darling," Margaret was saying when the telephone rang.

Aunt Gabbie, pronounced *Ont* not *Ant*, as Franny had been instructed to say, had called about Franny.

"Hello," Margaret said. "Yes, of course, Gabbie. I'm here in the kitchen, not working. Yes." Margaret nodded, rolling her eyes, as she listened to Gabriela speaking in her high soprano whine that everyone could hear across the room.

"Franny did have pain in the area of her appendix, Gabbie," she said, pausing to listen. "Of course I'm not lying. Why would I lie to you? Why would I lie at all? The pain just wasn't acute enough to warrant going to the hospital." Margaret pulled the phone cord and sat back down at the kitchen table. "Excuse me, Gabriela, but my sister, Estelle, is here from New York City so I need to ring off and call you back later."

"Dreadful woman," Estelle said. "In Denmark we execute women like that."

But Gabbie was still talking.

"No, no, no," Margaret interrupted. "That's not the case. The toilet paper incident was just an incident. Not a crushing psychological blow, Gabriela, honestly." She took a deep breath. "I must ring off now."

And she replaced the receiver on the hook.

"Why did you say I had appendicitis in the first place?" Franny asked. "Were you protecting me by lying?"

"A white lie," Margaret said. "I suppose I didn't want Gabbie to think you were fragile."

"I'm not fragile," Franny said crossly. "I stayed home from school because I wanted to stay home."

"I didn't want a fuss made about the toilet paper, darling, and Gabriela is such a busybody."

"Well, there *is* a fuss," Franny said, glad for a reason to storm out the kitchen door in front of Estelle, forgetting her coat, crossing the garden around to the front of the house to look out for Zeke, who would be coming home after tutoring in arithmetic.

She headed past the church to South Street where Zeke would be walking, suddenly desperate to see her little brother, just as he rounded the corner walking in her direction.

"Frannnnny," he called out and ran to her, flinging his arms around her waist. "You're out of your room. You're finally out of your room and I can see you again just like you used to be. Even your hair hasn't gotten any longer."

She lifted him in her arms, his skinny legs wrapped around her waist, his head resting in the V of her shoulder, tears gathering behind her eyes. Franny swallowed, determined not to cry, not now, not here in front of Zeke who would misunderstand her tears and think they were for sadness when they were tears of gratitude for the little boy, her brother, who had sat by her door day after day like a puppy, her very own puppy, loyal and true.

"You are my best friend in the world, Ezekiel S. Hall," Franny said, tickling him under the arms.

The sisters were poring over the letter to Signor Ferragamo when Franny returned with Zeke, Estelle on the telephone reading the sentences slowly one at a time.

"She's speaking to the Italian professor," Margaret said, bubbling with her familiar excitement. "Oh, Franny, this could be so fun — he's translating the letter for us."

Franny took milk out of the fridge and cookies for Zeke.

"What is going to be fun?" Zeke asked, settling down at the table next to Estelle.

"Maybe Franny and I will go to Italy where Salvatore Ferragamo makes shoes for famous people, and maybe he will be making your sister a pair of lovely shoes."

"And then she'll be famous?" Zeke asked, breaking his peanut butter cookies into so many little pieces.

"Not exactly," Franny said. "Then I'll have new shoes."

She grabbed a handful of cookies and headed up the stairs to her safe house where she sat on the bed with the lights out in her room, eating cookies in the early winter dark.

PLANS IN THE MAIL

Spring vacation was late that year, which was just as well since the weather for March was blustery and cold with more snow on the ground than there had been all winter. Sometimes the Halls went to Chicago for Easter to avoid the crowds at St. James Episcopal Church, staying at a hotel, ordering room service on Easter morning as a special treat. But this year Dr. Hall was too busy to leave. Terrance Flan, a boy in Zeke's class, was in the hospital with leukemia, and Mikey Houston's sister had been in an automobile accident on the way to Cleveland, breaking both of her legs.

"I can't possibly leave with so many children in the hospital," Dr. Hall told the family at dinner the week before Easter. "So Easter will be at our house with dyed eggs and rabbits and roasted lamb."

"I want to go to Chicago and have room service and television," Zeke said.

"Sorry, Zeke," Dr. Hall said. "I take care of my flock. That's the deal."

"What flock?" Zeke asked.

"The children of Easterbrook are my flock."

Later, after the dishes were done, the lights out in the kitchen, the family upstairs getting ready for bed, Zeke brought his copy of *Winnie-the-Pooh* into Franny's bedroom for her to read to him.

"Daddy's important in our town, isn't he?" Zeke asked.

"I think he is," Franny said, opening the first volume of *Pooh* to read again as she did almost every night. "A doctor is an important job."

"That's what I plan to be," Zeke said. "And when I get to be a doctor, I'll fix your foot and leg and stuff." He scrunched under the covers and leaned against Franny's arm.

"Thanks, Zeke, and then I won't have to worry about the stupid high school dances."

"I wonder why Daddy can't fix you up."

"I doubt I can be fixed or else he would have done it."

"He would have," Zeke said. "I know he would have fixed you 'cause he's our dad."

Franny had never thought about her father as a real person the way she thought about her mother. He was her father who loved her, mostly loved her, and he was strict and strong and a kind of hero in Easterbrook because he took care of children. But she had never wondered about him, the way she did about her mother, imagining Margaret Hall as a little girl. She'd never studied pictures of her father when he was young, as she did of her mother, thinking what she might have been like growing up as a teenager in Denmark.

Until very recently, her father had not been interesting to Franny, not as a person beyond his role as her father. When she moved into her bedroom after the Valentine's Dance, it had been the first time ever that her father had been angry at her. She could still hear him registering his displeasure, imagine him with narrowed eyes, his arms folded across his chest.

Once when she was younger, she had asked her mother *What do you love about Daddy?* since as far as Franny was concerned at the time, her mother was more exciting and beautiful to look at and warmhearted and interested in Franny than her father was.

"I love that he says what he thinks," Margaret Hall had said. "And does what he believes in."

"I guess that's true," Franny replied. "Sometimes I wish he'd keep what he thinks to himself."

"But someone who tells you what he thinks is a person you can trust," Margaret Hall had said.

"I suppose," Franny had said, misunderstanding her

father because he was often impatient and strict and severe. But lately, especially in the week she'd been alone in her room, she was beginning to understand the problems that come of being the person other people *want* you to be, as though it's their decision, as though they have control, as Franny had done in elementary school. And as Margaret Hall sometimes did with her *white lies*.

Of all the people Franny knew, only her father never cared what other people thought of him.

After she finished reading the chapter of *Winnie-the-Pooh*, Zeke slipped off her bed, holding up his too-big pajama bottoms with one hand, the other wrapped around *Pooh*.

"Do you like Mama and Daddy better than you did when you moved into your bedroom and locked the door?" he asked.

"Maybe and maybe not. I'll tell you in the morning, Ezekiel, but tonight, I'm too tired for a serious conversation."

But it wasn't tiredness she felt. Something stranger, more unfamiliar in herself. Sometimes for no reason at all she was angry. It just came over her as if she were boiling water. And then the gas under the pot of water turned off and the anger was gone.

She stretched out on her bed on top of the covers in the dark, wondering why out of nowhere she got suddenly angry not just at her parents or at her cousin Eleanor Hall, but at most of the freshman class at Easterbrook.

It was as if a dark and furious creature, a restless stranger had slipped under her old familiar skin.

"You're growing claws, Francine," Aunt Estelle had said to her at breakfast that day.

And Estelle was right. Franny was at war.

She'd arrive at school in the morning, her body arched for combat, hoping for trouble, ready for a fight as if every conversation with her friends or former friends was an attack she needed to defend against.

Most days she trolled through the list of the people she didn't like as if she were memorizing Latin verbs. Certainly she didn't like Estelle or Aunt Gabbie or Gabbie's husband, Uncle Tom Hall, or even their dog, Heather, who was a yappy cocker spaniel.

The only safe person in her life was Zeke and he wasn't even a full person. She thought of him as her devoted follower, the personal stuffed bear she hauled around under her arm.

Lying in the dark listening to the night sounds of the house, the traffic outside her window, choir practice letting out at the Episcopal church next door, she heard her mother's high heels clicking down the hall from Zeke's room to her room. There was a knock on the door and her mother opened it without an invitation.

The light from the hall spread over the covers of Franny's bed and she flung her arm across her eyes to keep it out.

"Franny?"

"I'm trying to sleep."

"What have you been saying to Zeke about us?" she asked.

"I don't remember every single thing I say to Zeke," Franny said. "Nothing terrible."

"Well, Zeke is a little boy who loves us and doesn't need to hear the remarks you make about his parents."

Her mother stood in the dark of the bedroom, backlit from the hall light, at a room's distance from Franny's bed looking very much like the outline of a tall scarecrow with her long legs and slender torso.

"I don't like this attitude you've developed that your father and I are less than human. I hope you understand what I'm talking about?"

Franny didn't reply.

"Of course you understand," her mother said and shut the door.

That night Franny couldn't sleep. She tried to read, turned out her light, and tried to fall asleep as she had always been able to do by staring at the church steeple outside her window until it faded to a pencil and disappeared. But finally she got up, took a shower, wrapped herself in a towel, and sat in bed with her writing notebook, filled with one and a half mystery novels written in longhand.

She had an idea for a new book.

Astrid and the Less-Than-Human Parents
Everyone in Granville where Astrid Noggin lived considered Astrid with her blonde curls and buck teeth and braces a perfectly normal twelve-year-old girl, a little smarter than the other girls in her class, except for the surprising fact that Astrid's parents, John and Ava Noggin, were donkeys. Regular-size thirty-five-year-old donkeys with gray hair and sticky-up ears and the stubborn bad temper of normal donkeys, except normal donkeys don't usually give birth to little girls.

She fell asleep in the middle of the first page, waking early, the bedside lamp still on, the notebook with the beginning of her new story lying on her belly, her body still wrapped in a towel.

The problem, at least the present problem, was Aunt Estelle.

Estelle had decided to extend her stay in Easterbrook for all of March, including spring vacation, while her husband finished his business in India. Now afternoons when Franny came home from school — and she had not missed a day of school for weeks — Estelle and Margaret were in the kitchen, drinking chocolate or hot tea or coffee with foamy milk and giggling. Even Estelle, serious, cantankerous Aunt Estelle, would be giggling sometimes uncontrollably into her teacup.

"Come sit with us," her mother would say when Franny walked into the kitchen after school.

But Franny didn't want to sit with them.

She'd shrug, open the door to the fridge or the cookie jar or the cupboard where crackers and bread were kept, fill the pocket of her winter jacket with treats, and go upstairs to her room. Sometimes she called Boots from the telephone in her mother's workroom and they would talk almost but not quite the way they used to talk before the Valentine's Dance.

"I guess you don't like Aunt Estelle either," Zeke said

one of the afternoons when he came in her room with his cars, zooming them across the carpet while she was trying to write.

"Not particularly."

"Because she's mean to you?"

"Because she's stupid," Franny said, happy with her choice of words. *Stupid* was not a word they were allowed to say in the Hall house and Zeke looked up at Franny with admiration.

"I don't like her either," Zeke added.

It was comforting that Zeke copied her feelings so she always had company in her sorrows.

"It's not that I dislike Estelle exactly. After all, she *is* our aunt," Franny said. "I just don't want to see her every day when I come home from school."

"Me neither," Zeke said, crawling up on her bed with his cars.

It was hard for Franny to hear the happiness between her mother and Aunt Estelle rolling out of the kitchen on the dark, late winter afternoons when she came home — Estelle sitting in the same blue straight-back chair where Franny used to sit with her mother after school.

Just the sound of their cheerful, chattering voices washed a wave of sadness across her afternoon.

It had been almost three weeks since the letter to Signor Ferragamo left in the post for Italy and though Franny did not expect a letter back, she was restless for news.

In the afternoon, walking home from school alone since she and Eleanor — with whom she had usually walked — were no longer best friends, she imagined the scene of excitement at the letter's arrival in the morning mail. She'd round the corner by the Episcopal Church and Margaret Hall would be waving from the front porch, a letter in her hand.

In Franny's daydreams, Aunt Estelle had returned to New York City with no plans in the future to come back to Easterbrook. Franny had her mother to herself again. She would follow Margaret Hall to the kitchen and they'd sit at the table together, drinking hot chocolate and reading the letter from Ferragamo.

"Signor Ferragamo says *COME* so we'll go," her mother would say. "Think of it, Franny! You'll be the only girl in Easterbrook EVER to go to Italy."

"When will we go?" she'd ask.

"We'll go immediately. Next week."

And every time she replayed the scene in her busy mind, Italy seemed more possible, an imagined tomorrow taking over the tedium of her daily life.

On the last day of school before Easter vacation, Franny ran into Mikey Houston on his bike coming from the hospital where his sister was being treated for her accident. He came to a screeching stop.

"So I hear from Eleanor that you're going to Italy for Easter break," he said.

"I am," Franny said, slinging her book bag over her shoulder.

"That's really neat," Mikey said. "You'll probably be the first kid in Easterbrook to meet the Pope."

"I'm not going to meet the Pope."

"That's all I know about Italy. My mom only thinks about the Pope," Mikey said.

"I don't know the Pope but in Florence there's a man who makes shoes for crippled girls. So!" She shrugged. "That's why I'm going to Italy."

Mikey Houston flushed bright red and hopped back up on his bike.

"See you," he called, standing up on the pedals, his head down. "I'm late getting home." And his tires squeaked as he went around the corner.

Franny turned at College Street. Way down the block at the other end of Scioto Street where her uncle and aunt lived, she thought she saw her cousin Eleanor in a bright green coat. Probably Mikey Houston was going to screech up next to her, slip off his bike, and tell Eleanor Hall about Franny's crippled feet.

She hated Mikey Houston.

Don't ever say hate, her mother had told her. *It's a dangerous word. Terrible things happen when we hate.*

So! She hated Mikey Houston and Eleanor Hall too.

Estelle and Margaret were in the kitchen as usual when Franny walked through the back door, hanging up her coat, picking up Pickle who was lying in the sun.

"Hi, darling," her mother said. "Aunt Estelle and I were talking about the letter to Signor Ferragamo."

"Is that all you talk about?"

"We have a lot of things we talk about that don't concern your feet, missy," Aunt Estelle said.

Franny opened the cookie jar. She had been eating way too many cookies lately, a small belly full of cookies making her jeans too tight. But she wanted one now.

Empty.

"Mama!"

"I'm so sorry, darling. I'll pick up some chocolate chips at the grocer later and make them tonight."

"Stop pandering to her, Margaret," Estelle said. "She doesn't even *speak* to you half the time."

She did speak to her mother, Franny thought. And she would talk to her all the time as she used to do if Estelle weren't sitting in the kitchen all day and all night taking up the oxygen.

She took out a carton of milk and poured Hershey's chocolate syrup into the bottom of a glass.

"If Francine wants to suffer, that's her choice," Estelle said. "She'll suffer whether she has cookies or not."

"I'm not suffering," Franny said, taking a box of crackers out of the cupboard, spreading them with peanut butter and marshmallow, making little sandwiches, thinking of suffering.

Was she suffering? Franny wondered. Was she feeling sorry for herself?

Don't feel sorry for yourself, darling, her mother had said to her recently. *It's a waste of time.*

"We were talking about Italy, darling," her mother was saying in that way she had of ignoring her sister's criticism as if she had not even heard it. "I have this bee in my bonnet."

"You ought to get rid of it," Estelle said.

"I have my fingers crossed that we're going to hear

from Signor Ferragamo soon, maybe in time to go to Italy for the week after Easter."

"This isn't useful, Margaret," Estelle said. "Franny?"

But Franny was already out the kitchen door and headed up the wide oak stairway with carved banisters and a spread of light through the stained-glass window at the landing, striping the stairs yellow and blue.

She sat on her bed, her legs crossed, the crackers in her lap, thinking of Mikey Houston. Certainly he would go straight home to tell his mom what Franny had said about her crippled feet.

After the ten o'clock Mass, Mikey's mom would report to everyone at coffee and donuts. The dreadful Aunt Gabbie would call Margaret Hall who would tell Dr. Henry Hall, and Franny would be required to apologize for being rude.

But it wasn't rude what she had said to Mikey Houston. It was the truth and he had been embarrassed to hear it, the way even her friends in elementary school had been embarrassed to mention Franny's crippled feet, sneaking a sideways glance at her, pretending as she had pretended, as her mother had insisted she pretend, that she was a perfectly normal, especially cheerful girl.

Besides, Franny thought, she certainly couldn't depend on Salvatore Ferragamo's letter inviting her to Florence. He probably wouldn't write back. When the letter from Margaret Hall arrived in Florence, Signor Ferragamo would glance at the return address, see that it came from Easterbrook, Ohio, and toss it in the wastebasket with the rest of the trash.

She lay down on her bed, her feet on the wall, staring at the ceiling. *Of course* she was feeling sorry for herself.

Zeke came home from school with chicken pox in little red blotches on his belly and arms. Just like Mikey Houston's pimples without the ooze.

"I don't have to go to school for two weeks," he said, walking into Franny's bedroom, where she lay on her stomach writing her book about Astril.

"Lucky you!"

"That's what Mama says. I'll get to do puzzles and make cookies and play cars all day with Mama and Aunt Estelle."

"The thing is, Zekey, it doesn't make a lot of difference to have chicken pox now because it's going to be spring vacation and we'll be out of school anyway." She sat up on her bed. "Maybe you can come to Italy with us."

"But I didn't think you wanted to go to Italy."

"I didn't," Franny said, moving over so Zeke and his cars could join her on the bed. "And I changed my mind."

But nothing happened spring vacation. Dr. Henry Hall spent every day and late into the evening at the hospital. Zeke's chicken pox got worse and then better and he stayed at home, mostly in the kitchen playing board games with his mother and Aunt Estelle. Estelle made no plans at all to go back to New York City.

"Is she moving *in* with us?" Franny asked her mother.

"No, but Uncle Douglas won't be home until the middle of April and she's having such a good time she's decided to stay," Margaret Hall said. "Why?"

"Because it doesn't even feel like our house any longer."

Most of spring vacation, Franny stayed in her room working on her new book. She made no plans to see her friends or go to the movies or hang out at the soda shop. Certainly she had no intention of going to the Sock Hop on the last Saturday of vacation.

No one, including her mother, even bothered to ask her if she was interested in going to the dance.

On the Saturday before Easter, a day Franny had dedicated to dyeing Easter eggs, drying them on towels on the kitchen table for the Easter Bunny in whom Zeke still had some faith, Mikey Houston's mother called.

Franny was late waking up, late for blueberry pancakes and bacon and hot chocolate. By the time she padded barefoot into the kitchen with a copy of "Astril," her mother was on the telephone speaking to Mikey Houston's mom.

"Thank you for letting me know," Margaret was saying as Franny came into the kitchen in her pajamas. "Of course Mikey was upset."

"Franny!" She replaced the receiver and sat down, her hands folded on the kitchen table. "What did you tell Mikey about Italy?"

"I told him the truth."

"But it upset him, darling," she said. "It made him uncomfortable and you never used to make your friends uncomfortable."

"So?"

"Aunt Gabbie called last night," her mother went on.

"I don't particularly like Aunt Gabbie so it doesn't matter to me what she says," Franny said.

She took a blueberry pancake from the plate and walked out the back door without a coat.

It was very cold, too cold to be walking around in flannel pajamas and slippers, but Franny sat down on the front step of the wraparound porch and hugged her knees to her chest against the bitter chill.

At St. James, choir practice for Easter Sunday was in full swing. Down the street, Mr. Goodly was sweeping the walk in front of his house and next door, Mr. Von Vleck, the mailman, was delivering mail to the Buckleys.

"What are you doing outside in your pajamas in this weather, Franny Hall?" Mr. Von Vleck asked, coming up the walk with a stack of mail held together in a rubber band in his hand. "Freezing to death is what you're doing!"

He gave her the mail.

"Two letters with foreign stamps and some bills," he said. "End of the month so the bills come."

"Thank you," Franny said pleasantly, putting the letters in her lap.

Her mother disliked the way the mailmen in Easterbrook checked the letters and let a person know what was in the mail before the person got to see for herself.

"Hope there's good news and someone sent you a dollar," Mr. Von Vleck said, coming down the steps.

Franny watched him walk down the path, past the Episcopal church, and across the street before she took off the rubber band and looked through the mail for herself.

There were bills as Mr. Von Vleck had said and a letter to her mother from her aunt Ele in Copenhagen and a postcard for Zeke from his friend Peter who had moved to Cleveland. Hi, Zeke. I got a new cocker spaniel called Woof. I have two friends at my new school. Love, Peter. There was a letter for Estelle from New York City and in the middle of all the bills, a thin letter postmarked *Firenze, Italia*.

The paper was crispy and so thin that Franny could fold it easily in fourths and stick it in the pocket of her pajama top, which she did. She put the rest of the mail in the mailbox on the front porch and walked around the house to the back door, through the door to the kitchen where her family, including Aunt Estelle who had come down to breakfast in her green terry-cloth robe and matching slippers, was finishing the blueberry pancakes.

"Ready for pancakes?" her mother asked brightly.

Franny picked up "Astril and the Less-than-Human Parents" and put the notebook under her arm.

"I'm not particularly hungry," she said, walking through the kitchen and up the back stairs to her bedroom.

BECOMING

Franny locked the bedroom door and climbed on her bed next to Pickle who was sleeping on her pillow, stretched out on his back, his paws over his ears.

Outside it was as cold and gray and gloomy as winter. Tomorrow the usual Easter egg hunts in the houses of Easterbrook would take place in the living rooms and dining rooms, the thermostats pushed up to seventy-five degrees. The pastel dresses passing by the Halls' house to St. James Episcopal Easter services would be covered by winter coats, some with velvet collars and leggings. The fathers would be wearing hats, the mothers gloves. Signs of spring were frozen mid-bloom on the yellow forsythia and the lavender crocuses, stunned and weepy in the front garden.

Just the day before, after school, while her mother was at the dentist with Zeke, the house empty, Franny had tried on a new pair of shoes, red leather with an open toe, which her mother had bought in Cleveland, shopping with Aunt Estelle. She sat at her mother's dressing table, put on the shoes, crossed her legs, and opened the drawer where Margaret Hall kept her makeup, applying rouge and powder, black mascara, blue eye shadow. She had crossed her right leg over her left so the especially skinny left leg was concealed and her feet, even open-toed, looked almost normal. She put on one of her mother's dresses with a circle skirt and tight waist. In the full-length mirror on the door, she had a sudden rush of pleasure.

There were two sheets of thin, crisp paper in the envelope from Italy, one handwritten in black ink in Italian, the second typed in English. She opened them on the quilt, pressing the paper flat.

Dear Margaret Hall,

It is my pleasure to offer to make your daughter's shoes from a last which I will create, fitting it exactly to her feet. For this, of course, you will make the trip to Firenze to my shop. I cannot assist with the cost of travel but will make this last without a charge. The shoes of course will be at a price to be determined. If this is an agreeable solution, please write to me again.

Yours truly,

Salvatore Ferragamo

Franny refolded the letter and put it in the top dresser drawer at the bottom under her sweaters.

She had been wrong. Aunt Estelle had been wrong. Only her mother, her stubborn, determined, optimistic mother, had known that Signor Ferragamo would write back with a plan.

When Zeke came into Franny's room with a basket of eggs to decorate for Easter, she was leaning against the quilted headboard of her bed, looking out the window at the heavy gray air, at the bare trees and the empty back porch of the Buckleys' house next door, weighted with winter sadness.

"I have brought eggs," Zeke said.

"So I see."

"They are for you to decorate. I'm not good at painting."

He took several pots of paint out of the basket.

"I have a good surprise," Zeke said, going to the sink, filling a pot with water to clean the brushes. "Aunt Estelle is leaving to go back to New York."

"That's very good news," Franny replied.

"She said she has outstayed her welcome."

"She's right about that."

Zeke climbed on the bed and scrunched in next to Franny.

"Mama and Aunt Estelle were having a fight about you."

"What about me?"

"About Italy."

He reached into the pocket of his flannel-lined jeans and took out a yellow marshmallow in the shape of a chicken from the package of Easter treats.

"Mama says you need to go to Italy to have a good life and Aunt Estelle says it's foolish to make you *special* and a stupidity for a girl your age to have fancy shoes and Mama said that you deserve fancy shoes and Daddy told Mama to calm down and that's when Estelle said she'd overstayed her welcome."

Franny was quiet, her back against the headboard, her legs crossed, her heart accelerating with a sudden flush of love for her mother, the way she used to feel about her when Margaret Hall was her best friend in all the world, her mother who had come again to Franny's defense the way she had always done all of Franny's life ever since she was born.

"That was extremely nice of Mama," she said.

"Yes it was, and it's very nice that Aunt Estelle is leaving for good. And also Daddy left the kitchen and said he had to go to work and Mama said, 'On Easter Saturday you're going to work?' and Daddy said, 'Kids get sick on Saturday just like every other day.'"

Zeke took the eggs out of the basket and put them on a towel.

"Can you help me paint the eggs now?"

"In a minute, Zekey."

"You promised me about the eggs."

"I will do the eggs with you," she said, and together they painted the Easter eggs and took them downstairs and Franny made herself a peanut butter and jelly sandwich and turned on the television.

"Aren't you supposed to be at a party today for Boots's birthday?" her mother asked.

"I said I couldn't come."

"Why did you say you couldn't when you can?"

"I just don't want to go," Franny said, her feet on the coffee table, the sandwich in her lap.

Her mother slipped down beside her on the couch, put her feet up next to Franny's, crossed her arms in that attitude she assumed when she wanted to talk about something important but didn't know exactly how to begin.

"What's going on with you, darling? You've been so, I don't know, so negative."

"I know," Franny said, going over to the TV to turn up the volume. "I don't know exactly why."

That night, after hot dogs and baked beans and *Maybe Tomorrow* on at eight on NBC, Franny read "Astril" to Zeke who thought it was a little boring and didn't like the donkey parents and wanted to read the chapter in *Winnie-the-Pooh* about Eeyore instead.

"'Astril' is a very good book, Zeke," she said crossly as he trotted off to bed. "You're just too young to understand it."

By the time Astril was fourteen, it was no longer amusing to have donkey parents as it had been when she was younger and her friends had come over to rub the donkeys' ears. Now Astril was embarrassed by her parents' donkey ways and heartsick that they had no idea about the true and pure feelings of a fourteen-year-old human girl, so they treated her like a donkey child, kicking her in the buttocks with their back legs, serving up hay and corn for dinner, spitting at her through their donkey teeth when she complained about her life.

She wanted a human boyfriend and ordinary parents to introduce to her friends and a house that didn't smell of hay and conversations at dinner that made her feel important as if she were the apple of their donkey eyes.

Alas for Astril Noggin, that was her fate and the only way she could escape it was to leave the Noggin house, maybe forever.

Franny finished writing "Astril" late, after her parents had gone upstairs to bed, the lights in the house out, Estelle on the telephone in the room next door speaking in Danish.

She was beginning to feel herself again, but not the old self of elementary school. It was as if she had lost touch with her best friend, and that friend who was herself, Franny/Francine Hall, had finally come home different than she'd been but also the same.

She put the notebook with "Astril" under her bed, took the letter from Signor Ferragamo out of her sweater drawer, wrote *SORRY FOR OPENING THIS FIRST* in ink across the open envelope, and stuck the letter under the door to her parents' room.

Three

FLIGHT INTO THE FUTURE

Franny stood with her mother at the United Airlines ticket counter in the Cleveland airport. Beside her, leaning against her hip, Zeke was crying. In a chair on the edge of the seating area, Dr. Henry Hall was reading the *Cleveland Plain Dealer*. Franny couldn't see his face.

"I think you're maybe going to die," Zeke said to no one in particular.

"We've no plans at all to die, my darling boy," Margaret Hall said. "We'll go to Florence for five days and then back to Easterbrook to you, my glorious child."

"I actually don't think it's a good idea for you to go on this plane," Zeke said. "It could rain."

Margaret Hall knelt beside him, took his face in her hands, and whispered something in his ear.

"What did she say to you?" Franny asked Zeke later, walking with him to the newspaper store for bubble gum, which she was glad to have since she doubted there was any gum on the plane for the stopped-up ears her mother had warned her about.

"She told me not to make you worried or you wouldn't go."

"I'm going. I told all the people at school that I was going so I'm not going to change my mind now."

On the Tuesday after Easter, Franny had arrived at school early, feeling better than she had since the day when she had tried on the silver shoes.

By second period, nearly everyone at Easterbrook High knew that Franny Hall was going to Florence, Italy, to meet Signor Ferragamo who was a shoemaker and would be making her new shoes.

People came up to her in the cafeteria and on the blacktop and at gym class. Even Mr. Hoagland, the principal, called her into his office to say how thrilling it was that Franny would be the first student at Easterbrook to travel to the continent.

Eleanor met her in front of the school waiting by a lamppost.

"I can't believe you're going to Italy and skipping school," she said.

Eleanor looped her arm through Franny's as if they were still friends.

"You never even mentioned it at our house on Easter Sunday."

"The letter came the day before Easter but I didn't know whether I'd be able to go."

"And now you'll get these regular shoes and you'll just be normal, right? That's what your mom told my mom."

"I'll have new shoes, regular shoes like every other girl in town," she said.

Franny didn't know about *normal*. Certainly Signor Ferragamo, however miraculous he was with shoes, couldn't make her normal. Even a surgeon accustomed to remaking bones could not do that. But she hadn't allowed herself to think about meeting Signor Ferragamo, only the trip to Italy, only the chance she now had at Easterbrook High to be noticed because she was skipping school to go on a romantic adventure.

But to imagine *normal* was too chancy.

They walked to Main Street.

"Want to get a soda?"

"I can't," Franny said. "We've got too much to do."

"I've been meaning to ask, are you still mad at me about Mikey?"

"I wasn't mad about Mikey," Franny said, slipping her hands into the pockets of her jeans.

She might have said more. She might have said that the girls in Easterbrook with their boyfriends and cliques and competition for cheerleader and stupid dances made her feel worse about herself than she already did.

Instead she turned left on Main away from the square and waved good-bye to Eleanor, a cheerful wave that she invented for the occasion.

Maybe someday she would have somebody in her life, a Mikey Houston or better. But she wasn't going to hold her breath, as her father would say.

Heading home, she almost missed the turn on College Street, so busy picturing the next time she saw her cousin, Eleanor Hall.

It would be a Monday, the day after she got home from Italy with her new shoes like the penny loafers that Eleanor was wearing with knee socks and short corduroy skirts, the uniform of every other girl in high school.

Franny would meet Mikey Houston at the soda shop before school and they'd walk hand in hand up Main Street toward the high school when Eleanor turned the corner, coming from the other direction.

"Hiya." Franny would wave to Eleanor, without stopping to talk.

And as they passed Eleanor on the street, Franny would kiss Mikey Houston on the lips.

Over and over, she played that scene in her mind, like a television commercial, always exactly the same.

Zeke had been inconsolable, his head down on his knees, sobbing into his woolen pants until the loudspeaker called out their United flight to New York City connecting at Idlewild Airport for Rome, stopping in Gander, Newfoundland, to refuel.

Zeke stood up then, wiped his eyes with his shirt, stuffed his small hands into the pockets of his pants, and said good-bye.

He didn't even look at Franny when she kissed him and would not kiss his mother good-bye or wait with Dr. Henry Hall to see his family on the plane. He turned and headed in the direction of the parking lot.

"Will Zeke be okay?" Franny asked her mother.

"Of course," Margaret Hall said. "He'll be fine."

But Franny had a sudden, unexpected misgiving as if without her, life in Easterbrook was at risk, especially for

Zeke. Even Pickle's cat life hung in the balance without Franny to watch over him.

In the plane, her seat belt fastened, her eyes fixed on the stewardess as she detailed the safety measures to be taken in the event of an emergency, Franny was suddenly weightless. The plane's clattering propellers whirled into motion, and the plane sailed them down the runway and up into the gray Ohio sky. Below, the tiny houses and acres of fields spread like a toy village, and they disappeared under the clouds so that all Franny could see was white, white under the plane and over it, as if the life she'd left was really invisible and only she and her mother were real.

Dear Zeke, she wrote on the F-initial stationery she'd bought at Fuller's just for the trip. I'm in New York City now, actually in the airport where I've met a little girl gypsy with her mother. It is the little girl's job to go up to strangers with her big, sad eyes and beautiful curls and say to them in English (I don't know what language gypsies speak), "Please can you give money. We have no food."

Mama said "absolutely no" money for the gypsy girl and gave her a chilly look. But I took out a dollar and the little girl was all over me, stuck like a leech, and then the mother gypsy came and took my purse. The police said they could do nothing and I was wrong to give out money to the gypsies but luckily she only got the purse without my passport or money, which are in my backpack. We're heading to Italy in about half an hour. I wish Mama would consider adopting this adorable girl so she could have a normal life. Perhaps you could mention it to Dad. I love you forever and a day, JH

Dear Boots, Franny wrote, sitting on the hard seat in the airport at Gander, Newfoundland, where the plane was held for an undetermined amount of time until the weather cleared. I'm in Newfoundland and we're stuck here because of storms. It's strange. There's nothing here. I feel as if we've landed on the moon. I'll be in Rome tomorrow. Tell Mikey the Pope's very busy but sends his best wishes to Mikey's mom. I met someone from Florence on the plane from New York to Newfoundland, but he doesn't speak English. I like to think he said we may go to the movies when I get to Florence but I'm not at all sure. He could have said anything and I wouldn't know the difference. Love, Franny

Dear Eleanor,

The trip from Gander to Rome was horrible. The plane felt like a toy tossing and turning, sinking several feet down in a squish so I felt as if I'd left my stomach in the air. A lot of people threw up but I didn't and nor did my mom. It became a matter of principle. Mama said, "If you throw up, you owe me dinner when we get to Florence." And I said, "If you throw up, you owe me an Italian sweater." When we landed in Rome, it was so foggy that we saw nothing until BOOM, we were on the ground with a bang and a shudder. I met one guy when we were in Gander. His name is Mario and he's Italian and lives in Rome and had been in Cleveland visiting colleges for next year because his aunt and uncle live in Cleveland. Italian guys our age are much more grown-up than the guys at Easterbrook. Hope you're having fun with Mikey. See ya, Franny

Dear Zeke, **Franny wrote in the train station after they had gone through customs in Rome and taken a taxicab to the train station and were waiting for the train to Florence.** I love Rome. It's very beautiful and big and Italian. I keep thinking about the gypsy girl and wishing we could bring her home. I'm having a wonderful time and missing you too. Love and hugs, F

If she were to write to her father next and tell him the truth about the trip to Florence, the absolute truth without any fabrications, she would have said she was scared almost to death after the wild ride from Gander to Rome and the gypsy girl and the pushing and shoving in the airport in Rome and the fight for the taxi and the Italians screaming in Italian and then more pushing and shoving in the station in Rome, everyone rushing to get somewhere, to knock someone out of line, racing to the train, throwing their luggage through the windows, climbing through the windows themselves, to get there first, to find a seat. It was crazy and Franny wasn't at all sure she was going to make it back to Easterbrook alive.

She folded her letter to Zeke and put it in an envelope in her bag with the other letters, leaning against the back of the hard bench, waiting for the train to Florence. Margaret Hall was sitting next to her, her legs crossed, her slender hands loosely folded on her lap, her eyes closed, a tiny smile on her lips. She seemed to be sleeping, although when Franny touched her hand, touched the blue protruding vein on her mother's hand, thinking as she did how vulnerable her mother seemed in the artificial lights of the station, she opened her eyes.

"Almost," she said. "Almost there."

SIGNOR SALVATORE FERRAGAMO

Franny and her mother had a room that had been arranged by Signor Ferragamo at a pensione next to the Spedale degli Innocenti, which was a hospital for foundlings.

The pensione, built in 1445 around the same time as the foundling hospital, had been a private home but was now residential apartments built around a courtyard.

It was the hospital for foundlings that caught Franny's attention, the first place she saw when the taxi from the train station dropped them off at the pensione.

"Foundlings?" she asked.

"Orphans," her mother told her. "Abandoned babies used to be left between the figures of Mary and Joseph. I looked it up in the guidebook."

"Because they were sick babies?"

"Maybe, or maybe the parents couldn't afford to take care of them."

There were round ceramic medallions made by Andrea della Robbia, each with a fat little baby in swaddling clothes against a bright blue background, and somehow these adorable infants were a solace to Franny so far away from home. A place for babies for hundreds of years. Even now she would find a measure of safety here.

Walking across the courtyard next door to the hospital, to check into their room on the second story of the pensione, Margaret slipped her hand in Franny's, shyly, perhaps expecting Franny to shake loose her hand.

"Are you getting to be glad you came?" she asked.

"Glad at least not to be in Easterbrook."

"It's pretty here, don't you think? Just here in this lovely courtyard."

"It's pretty," Franny agreed.

Their room was a bedroom with a shared bath in an apartment belonging to a young Italian and his wife. The family was called del Santo and according to Signor del Santo who spoke a little English, they had a nephew, Filippo, who lived with them and was an "arteest" and spoke English, and a little girl who was "six."

"Six?" Margaret Hall asked.

"Seek," Signor del Santo said, shaking his head.

"I think he means sick," Franny said to her mother.

But neither the nephew, Filippo, nor the little girl seemed to be at the apartment when the Halls arrived.

Signor del Santo took their luggage to the bedroom, a spare simple room with a large window overlooking the courtyard. He indicated the bathroom across the hall.

"Only one," he had said, pointing to them and then to himself. "You first." He smiled.

Signora del Santo was a tall, slender woman, taller than her round sweet-faced husband, quiet, a little grim, but she was curious about Franny's crippled leg.

"She's staring at me," Franny said to her mother as they climbed into bed the first night.

Margaret Hall shrugged.

"Some people are afraid of differences in others and maybe Signora del Santo is one of those people. I wouldn't worry."

Somehow she had expected a certain tolerance in Florence that she didn't find in Easterbrook or Cleveland or Toledo or even New York City.

"I wish people would look at my face instead of my leg," she said.

"It's a beautiful face," her mother said.

"But people's eyes always wander straight to my leg."

"That will change," her mother said.

Franny didn't disagree. She didn't believe her mother, didn't believe she would ever escape the stares of strangers, but sometimes it wasn't worth it to object to Margaret Hall's determined hope for things to be different.

On their first morning in Florence, the day they were to meet with Ferragamo, they walked down the stone steps of the pensione and across the courtyard, glancing up at the apartment where Signor and Signora del Santo were drinking their coffee on the balcony, the shutters of their living room open although the weather was quite cool.

They had taken a seat at a small table in the café across the courtyard when a sound came from the open window of the del Santos' apartment.

"What a strange loon-like sound," Margaret Hall said. "Like a child."

"Whatever is making that noise, the del Santos are still sitting on the balcony acting as if it's perfectly normal," Franny said.

Margaret looked up.

"Maybe it's their sick child."

The day was sunny and blue, the courtyard bustling with children in brown uniforms on their way to school, the sounds of their high-pitched voices like birdcalls in the soft Florentine air.

A tall, slender man, maybe younger than a man but no longer a boy, came down the steps from the pensione and strode across the courtyard into the café, picked up a newspaper, and ordered a coffee. Close up, Franny guessed he was about eighteen, with straight black hair worn long, over his ears, and olive skin, high cheekbones, a seriousness about him. Franny watched him out of the corner of her eye. The second time the "loon" sound came from the del Santos' open window, he glanced up and shook his head, saying something in Italian to the waiter, whom he seemed to know.

"Pretty boy," Margaret Hall said, looking up from the fashion magazine she had taken from her satchel, always carrying the new issue of one or another fashion magazine.

Pretty boy was her mother's term for handsome.

Margaret Hall sat at an angle, her legs crossed, her head turned in such a way that seemed posed, glancing at the young man.

"What are you thinking?" she asked.

"I'm thinking about that little girl," Franny said.

"And the boy with a newspaper?" her mother said.

"Man with a newspaper."

"No, he's a boy worth thinking about!"

They ordered another coffee and biscuits, unaccustomed to such a small breakfast.

The boy uncrossed his legs, stretched them out in front so his feet touched the leg of Franny's chair and she could no longer see his face, which was covered by the newspaper.

"I'm so glad you were willing to come with me, Franny," Margaret was saying.

"As if you would have come *without* me?"

Her mother laughed.

"I wouldn't have come at all, of course."

"I don't want to hurt your feelings about this trip, Mama, but I came with you because I had told my friends at Easterbrook that I was coming," Franny said. "That's all. I am not particularly interested in the shoes."

"Of course, darling," Margaret said. "And I came because Signor Ferragamo is a gift who dropped in our laps from heaven."

Franny shrugged.

She wasn't thinking about shoes. She didn't want sightseeing or conversations with Signor Salvatore Ferragamo. She didn't want to go to dances in Easterbrook any more than she had ever wanted dances. If anything, she simply wished her mother had brought her to Italy for the fun of it. Just the fun of it.

But here they were sitting in a small café near an old hospital drinking very black and muddy coffee waiting for eleven o'clock.

"We'll see Signor Ferragamo and then we'll look around Florence and go to dinner and then back here."

Margaret looked over at Franny, who had slid down in her chair and was sitting with her long hair more or less spread across her face like a scarf.

Although it was too late for a reversal of plans, Franny wondered, should she tell her mother that she had never wanted to have shoes made in the first place? That she hadn't mentioned a desire for shoes, not even the ill-fated silver shoes stuffed with toilet paper? These choices all began with her mother's longings and not her own.

She had come to Italy to escape the humiliations of high school. To be a girl, unlike every other girl at Easterbrook High, who got to go to Italy to have her shoes made. If only she could forget the part about the shoes.

When Franny got up to leave, the child — if it was a child — was making soft, irritable meows from the second floor of the pensione, and the del Santos were still sitting in the open window with their coffee as if it were a perfectly normal morning and the crying was music to their ears.

"I think I'm going back to my room to change." Franny hoped the boy with a newspaper didn't see her limp out of the café.

What else would he notice but her damaged leg and orthopedic shoes?

Another couple in the café had summoned a waitress and, pointing to the del Santos' apartment, must have asked what was going on with the child.

The waitress shook her head, moving her hands back and forth to indicate *"No, no, no,"* she would not answer. It was none of their business.

Walking alone across the courtyard, stepping cautiously over the uneven cobblestones, Franny felt a sudden surge of independence.

She saw herself at a distance, alone in a strange city without the language to negotiate its streets, and at that small moment a sense of her own future was like the taste of honey on her tongue.

She could live in Florence in the del Santos' pensione.

She would find a way to befriend the boy in the café, maybe work in the café as a waitress.

Dear Eleanor, she would write to her cousin. *I have decided to stay in Florence, tired of high school, tired of Easterbrook. But really I'm staying because I have a job and a new boyfriend and sometime I'll probably come home, but I read in one of my mother's magazines about a girl who went to Chile to live for a while and skipped high school and went straight to college. Hope you and Mikey are great. FH*

Franny walked up the marble steps to the second floor of the apartment and knocked on the del Santos' door, walking in without waiting for someone to answer. The child was crying still but softly with short gasps and Franny could tell that the sounds came from behind the closed door to the next room.

She went to her room, hung up two skirts in the narrow closet, crossed the hall to the bathroom, splashed water on her face, and put her hair in a soft bun on top of her head so her face looked thinner and older.

She said hello to the del Santos, now in the kitchen, Signora del Santo washing up, Signor del Santo ready to leave for work in his cap and jacket.

He smiled and Signora handed Franny a ripe brown and yellow pear.

"Sit," Signora del Santo said, pointing to the kitchen table.

Franny sat on the edge of a wooden chair.

"Will I get to meet the baby?" Franny asked.

"Ana Maria seek."

She pointed to her head to indicate the head was Ana Maria's problem.

"Later maybe," Franny said, "when I get back from my appointment."

Signora del Santo smiled.

"*Sì, sì,*" she said. "Later, later . . ."

From the window of their bedroom, Franny watched her mother walk across the courtyard. She liked to watch her mother in high heels, more like an athlete than a model, although she looked prettier to Franny than the models in the magazines her mother loved to look at. She had a long stride, swinging her arms, her body like a dancer's in its grace, and she walked quickly unless she was next to Franny, who could not move fast enough to keep up.

Halfway across the courtyard, Margaret Hall was talking to an older man in a suit, small, with gray curly hair, a newspaper under his arm. Franny couldn't see his face.

Her mother reached in her purse, took out something, perhaps a map, and they looked at it together, speaking easily back and forth so he must have spoken English. Her mother touched his shoulder as they parted, waved upstairs probably to Signora del Santo, and Franny heard her high heels clicking along the ceramic tile floor of the del Santos' apartment.

"Hello, darling." She dropped her purse and the Italian fashion magazine on the bed. "We have to leave soon. It's just after ten and I don't know how long the walk to Ferragamo's will take us."

"Who was that man you were talking to?" Franny asked, dropping onto the bed, the exhaustion of travel overtaking her.

"Dr. Vincente."

"Did he speak English?"

"A bit. He's a doctor who knows the del Santos so I asked him about the child." She pulled the sweater she was wearing over her head. "He told me she was injured from a fall out of the window, and she is deaf, so she doesn't know the sounds she makes."

"Fell out of this apartment?"

"And onto the courtyard." Her mother checked through the clothes still folded in her suitcase, taking out a navy blue double-breasted jacket. "And that boy with the newspaper, you know."

"I remember," Franny smiled.

"Well, he is Filippo, the del Santos' nephew, so he lives here."

She slipped out of her trousers and shook out a straight skirt.

"With us?"

She nodded.

"Signor Vincente showed me the directions to Ferragamo's on the map. He said the shop is fancy so I'm changing to something dressier."

"What about me?"

"You could wear the dress I got you, the jumper with my Chinese jacket that Uncle Douglas brought me the last time he was in China."

"So she fell out of the window when?" Franny asked.

"Just after she learned to walk."

"And how come they keep her in that room?"

"Signor Vincente says they are ashamed that she fell out the window," Margaret said, slipping the pencil skirt over her head.

"Is that weird?"

"Not if you're a parent, darling. You blame yourself."

Franny changed to a thin wool herringbone jumper with a scooped neck, sleeveless, and she wore it with a blouse.

"Do you want any makeup?" her mother asked.

"You only have mascara."

"I brought lipstick in case you wanted it."

"This isn't exactly a fashion show, is it?"

Franny had a picture in her mind of slender crepe-paper models, their arms raised above their heads, their bodies twisted like dancers, their shoes with twig-thin heels and sprinkled with jewels. A picture like the ones she'd seen in her mother's stack of issues of *Vogue* magazine.

"Do you own any pairs of Ferragamo's shoes?" Franny asked as they went down the marble stairs to the courtyard.

"Only movie stars own Ferragamo shoes in the United States."

"Movie stars, models, and me," Franny said. "This is crazy."

Her mother laughed.

"Too late, darling. We're committed."

They walked across the courtyard and up the narrow streets to the Duomo, the green, white, and pink marble façade shimmering in the sunlight.

"Are we going in?" Franny asked.

"Later when we have more time," her mother said, turning toward the Piazza Santa Maria Novella with its gothic church.

Franny slipped her arm through her mother's to keep her balance on the cobblestone streets, and Margaret read from the guidebook she was following, pointing out this church and that palace as they walked by the old cemetery next to the basilica.

They headed toward the River Arno to the end of the Via de' Tornabuoni, where the shop of Salvatore Ferragamo was located in the Palazzo Spini Feroni, a large palace bought by Ferragamo in 1938 after he left Hollywood and returned to Italy to set up shop in Florence.

Franny was struck by the way the women on the street were dressed, the boxy jackets and short skirts on the square-shaped women, high heels, no jewelry, little makeup. Always a scarf with the orange earth tones of the Florentine landscape as if these women were in uniform, but elegant in a way that Franny had never seen in Easterbrook except with her mother.

The palace was on the street with a very narrow sidewalk facing the river.

In order to gain access, Margaret Hall rang a doorbell and waited.

"Why would they have a doorbell to get into a store?"

"It's a specialty store."

"A rich store?"

"An Italian store."

The man who answered the door was small with an impressive hooked nose and very thin, wearing a gray suit that fit him *like a glove*, Margaret said.

"It's way too tight," Franny said later to her mother. "I could see *everything* as if he were naked, and when he sits down, it'll rip in the seat."

He introduced himself as Signor Strolla and did not extend his hand.

"We're here to see Signor Salvatore Ferragamo," Margaret said coolly, as if nothing in the grandeur fazed her as it did Franny. "I am Margaret Hall from the

United States and Signor Ferragamo is expecting us." She turned to Franny. "This is my daughter, Francine."

"Yes," Signor Strolla said. "Come in."

He stepped aside.

The store was nothing like a shop or a city store, which was what Franny knew of glamorous in Cleveland, Ohio. It was more like a stage set. A very large room with marble floors, walls painted with frescoes of landscapes, a painting of a contemporary Madonna in a gold frame.

There were very few shoes. At least very few were on display. Four pairs, each arranged on its own pedestal built in the shape of a column. The furnishings were spare — a long, narrow wood table in the middle of the room, a pair of lavender shoes displayed next to a tall silver vase with a single white rose on a crimson scarf, a brown velvet couch with a curved back and carved wood with silk pillows, two on the couch, some on the floor. And high-back chairs in which elegant women were sitting dressed as if they were going to a tea dance or a funeral, or maybe the Halls had arrived in the middle of a play.

The room was hushed, almost soundless.

"I'm bolting," Franny whispered as the man in the tight suit scanned the room, looking just beyond the Halls as if they were not quite important enough to look at directly.

Her mother shot Franny a look that said, *Too late to change your mind now!* and *Get hold of yourself* and *Don't ruin this morning!*

Franny considered the long walk on marble between the entrance door and the empty velvet chairs to which Signor Strolla gestured. Everyone in the room would stare at her when they heard the sound of her shoes on marble. They'd raise their eyebrows.

She was flushed with shame. Her heavy shoes, like the metal-shod hooves of a horse, clomped across the room, hammering the marble with every uneven step, *like a rhinoceros*, she said later to her mother, limping past the long, thin models and the movie stars with fleshy breasts.

"Please make yourself at ease." Signor Strolla bowed slightly in his tight suit. "Signor Ferragamo will be here presently."

"I don't think I've ever felt more ugly in my lifetime of ugliness," Franny whispered to her mother.

She sat down in a chair high off the ground with a curved springy velvet seat and arms, feeling square and uncomfortable.

She was in the process of turning into a freak. She could feel it happening inside out, feel herself growing wider and wider, her hips spreading until they fell Jell-O-like off the sides of the plushy chair. Her face was exploding in blemishes, her herringbone jumper with the puffy-sleeved blouse made her look like a bowl of mayonnaise. She could hear her hair frizz as if it had received an electrical shock, her eyebrows spread across her forehead forming a single thick black line over her eyes.

Any moment, the ocean of tears forming behind her eyeballs from sheer frustration and embarrassment was going to spill down her cheeks.

"Who *are* these people?" Franny asked. "It feels as if I'm the freak in a movie."

Her mother leaned slightly forward so she wouldn't need to raise her voice.

"The woman in gray," her mother said close to her ear, "the one with near shaved hair and that blanket which is supposed to be a coat, is probably modeling the alligator shoes she's wearing for the movie stars sitting around the room waiting to see Signor Ferragamo." She patted Franny's knee. "But he'll see us first."

"I want to go home."

By home she meant Easterbrook, not the apartments next to the foundling hospital.

This trip had been a terrible mistake.

"I think the woman in fuchsia is also a model," her mother continued. "And she's walking back and forth in front of those two actresses — they have to be actresses in their nightgown dresses with all that costume jewelry — modeling those gold strappy shoes that only a greyhound puppy has thin enough ankles to wear."

"I'm only interested in leaving this place right now," Franny said in a stage whisper.

In her mind, Franny was negotiating with the God of the Episcopalians next door to their house in Easterbrook or the Fates or the heroes of Greek mythology who lived on Mt. Olympus, the ones she'd loved in eighth grade.

So listen, God, Franny was saying to herself. *I promise to forget these high-top oxfords with the big lift. I'll never complain again and if you'll be good enough to get me out of here and home, I'll even go to the dances.*

She took a deep breath.

Not all the dances but let's say one, maybe even two a year and I'll wear the orthopedic shoes and go to Cleveland with my mother to buy formal dresses for the dances if you'll just make it possible for me to leave immediately by train or taxicab for Rome.

Her mother had taken down the lavender shoes on the long table and was trying one of them on her left foot.

So, God, the only way to accomplish this is to approach my mother with a problem. Maybe a thunderstorm or a tornado or World War III could start immediately in Florence so we'd be in an emergency situation and have to leave. Amen, she added, hoping that would help.

Her mother was replacing the lavender shoe on the top of the column where it had been displayed.

"I'm exploding," Franny said in a stage whisper. "And you'll be humiliated if you're sitting here with me when I erupt."

The models wandered around the room, winding in and out among the chairs, some with clients, actresses, young wealthy women, an elderly woman too old to buy new shoes with her assistant.

"I feel like a pound dog, Mama," Franny said. "Like I might as well tear off my clothes and sit naked while everyone pretends not to notice but *is* actually noticing that I have pimples the size of marshmallows all over my face."

"Your face isn't breaking out, Franny, and I don't even think anyone notices that you're here. They're all too involved with themselves."

"They notice. I am going to be personally responsible for the end of Signor Ferragamo's shoe business."

Franny had never felt so exposed. At the Valentine's Dance, she had been humiliated among friends who had formed better opinions of her in elementary school, and those opinions could not have been completely *ruined* by the toilet paper incident no matter how awful it had been.

Here she was among strangers staring at her under their liquid-shadowed eyelids, no doubt wondering what so homely a girl in such clunky shoes and a deeply ugly jumper was doing in Florence, Italy, at the elegant shop of Salvatore Ferragamo.

The question she was considering was whether to leave the shop immediately and get lost in Florence without a word of Italian except *sì* and *no*. Or to stay and die of humiliation.

But just as Franny had decided to bolt, Salvatore Ferragamo burst into the front door of the shoe shop and hurried across the marble floor.

"Buongiorno," he said gruffly, his arms extended in a gesture of hello.

"Francine," he said as if he had known her for years. "My child, my daughter, my heart."

And he kissed her hand. All around the room, the elegant long-necked women turned their swan heads toward the cheerful commotion.

POSSIBILITIES

Margaret pushed open the heavy door to Ferragamo's and walked onto the narrow sidewalk across the street from the Ponte Vecchio as the cars whipped by, close enough to touch.

"That was amazing," she said.

Franny, shivering in the cool, damp air of early spring, pressed her fists into the pockets of her jacket.

"He just loved you, Franny."

Franny hardly knew what to say.

"Didn't you think he was wonderful?" Margaret grabbed Franny's elbow, dashing across the street between the cars thundering in their direction.

"Aren't you glad we came?" she asked.

Franny stepped onto the curb, moving into the busy pedestrian traffic, away from the cars.

"You're so quiet, darling."

"I just am," Franny said, too bewildered by what had happened, how unexpected Signor Ferragamo had been with her, uncertain of what to say.

Margaret pulled her toward her, kissed the top of her head.

"Of course, darling," she said. "It wasn't at all what I had expected."

The picture in Franny's mind was the look on the faces of the women, the models and actresses and wealthy women dressed off the pages of *Vogue* magazine, when Salvatore Ferragamo rushed in the room and kissed her on both cheeks, both cheeks the way her mother did, *as if we were related.*

"Did you notice the look of astonishment on the faces of those terrible women when he kissed you?"

And Franny smiled.

They pushed into the middle of the crowds, finding space to squeeze in two abreast.

"Sal-va-tore Fer-ra-gamo," Margaret sang.

"Mama!"

"No one speaks English."

"Salvatore Ferragamo? They'll understand it when you sing his name."

Margaret led Franny out of the crowds of people shopping midday, taking her in the direction of the stores.

"Tell me you're glad you came," she said, "and not just

to be free of your class at Easterbrook but to be here with me and Signor Ferragamo."

"I'm glad for today," Franny said, leaning into her mother's shoulder. "He made me feel like a giant."

Margaret laughed. "Not a giant. A princess."

"A wealthy princess."

"A movie star."

"Marilyn Monroe."

"Not Marilyn Monroe," Margaret said. "June Allyson."

"Marlene Dietrich." Franny struck a pose, an invisible cigarette between her lips.

They pushed through the crowd of tourists to the bridge.

The Ponte Vecchio was a bridge over the River Arno with jewelry and leather in tiny shops with large windows lining either side of the bridge. Franny and Margaret walked along the bridge, looking at the shops on one side and crossing to the other, passing by kiosks of leather and Florentine paper, religious artifacts, scarves, and jewelry from goldsmiths and silversmiths, cameos set in earrings and necklaces and bracelets, white raised figures, usually with the head of a woman against a sepia background.

Franny chose one for her grandmother Hall, a bracelet for herself and one for Boots. At her mother's insistence she added one for Eleanor.

She had not discussed Eleanor's betrayal with her mother. Already Margaret Hall was too involved in Franny's life to tell her about crushes and daydreams and boyfriends who would never turn out to be real.

"I'm sort of *done* with Eleanor," she told her now. "She's not been a good friend. Just a cousin I didn't choose to have."

"What did she do?" Margaret asked.

"Just stuff, Mama. Girls' stuff."

Although it struck Franny that Eleanor had not done anything so terrible. How was she to know that Franny's mind was full of pictures of Mikey Houston, of dancing with Mikey, sharing a root beer float at the soda shop, walking hand in hand down College Street?

She hadn't thought about Mikey Houston once since she'd left Ohio, not even on the plane when she had nothing but time to think.

"What should we get for Aunt Estelle?" Margaret was searching through the silver jewelry. "Not the cameos. Her taste is too plain for cameos."

"I suggest nothing," Franny said.

Her mother had picked up a wide silver cuff and was trying it on her wrist.

"What's your problem with Estelle, Franny?"

"I got to dislike her after she had been staying with us for about four hundred days."

"A month." Margaret purchased the bracelet for Estelle although she continued to wear it on her own wrist.

"It felt like forever."

Margaret shrugged.

"Estelle's a little pushy but she is my sister and I love her."

"She has too many opinions," Franny said.

Franny was unwilling to admit she'd been jealous of Estelle settled at the kitchen table, stealing her mother, leaving Franny with a sick longing in her stomach and a bad temper as Estelle and her mother giggled over tea and secrets every afternoon.

Maybe she would say nothing. Estelle was in New York. Franny was in Italy and the sun above them was brilliant, almost warm. Her heart was racing with happiness.

"I love Florence," she said, picking out a leather box she'd fill with Italian currency for Zeke and a bright blue silk tie for her father.

Margaret was trying on a leather jacket.

"What do you think?" she asked.

"You look like a motorcycle driver from Akron," Franny said. "Sort of tough."

"That's because in America, only motorcyclists wear leather. In Europe, women think it's feminine and elegant."

She bought the jacket, folded it into her satchel.

"What do you think, Franny? Would you wear this in Easterbrook?"

"Not a chance," Franny said.

"Well, I will."

Their satchels full, they wandered along the River Arno toward the Uffizi Gallery and the Piazza della Signoria where Margaret wanted to see the replica of Michelangelo's statue of the *David*.

Franny had seen the picture in the guidebook of *David* with his big head and long arms, but she had never been to a gallery except once to the Metropolitan in New York with Estelle, who insisted that she see the Impressionist painters with their fuzzy blue paintings and the mummy collection and Egyptian artifacts, and wouldn't stop for lunch in the cafeteria. So Franny associated art with hunger and on a second trip had refused to go to the Museum of Modern Art in favor of ice skating with her father.

"David of David and Goliath," Margaret said, slipping her arm through Franny's. "I wish I'd taught you the stories in the Old Testament."

The only sculpture Franny knew was the small statue of Benjamin Wicks, born and died in Easterbrook, Ohio, honored as a native son with a statue in the center of the square for inventing something having to do with grain mills.

"There he is," Margaret Hall said, slipping into the crowd surrounding Michelangelo's *David* looming above them, sunlight glittering across his broad face, his marble curls, the enormous muscles of his arms.

Franny stood back, away from the tourists as they moved in a slow circle around the statue, their heads turned upward toward his face, conscious of her own heartbeat.

Something in the size of the sculpture stirred and excited her, in the raw force of the *David*, as if in his stillness, he were about to burst out of his marble body into the crowd surrounding him.

Her mother kept art books and loved looking at them almost as much as her fashion magazines, so Franny had seen a photograph of *David* and other sculptures, paintings, and buildings, including the Duomo and Ghiberti's bronze doors. But standing in the piazza, less anonymous among these strangers than she sometimes felt at home, a new future suddenly seemed possible. Not in a particular way, but it was as if there was an air bubble of possibility in her bloodstream.

Since the Valentine's Dance, she had been in the process of becoming *somebody* beyond her parents' belief in her or Zeke's dependence or her own limited sense of the girl she'd been in elementary school.

Walking along the river, across the bridge, Franny and Margaret wandered through the Boboli Gardens on a hillside overlooking Florence, lacing their way through gardens of statues and obelisks and benches where they lay, the sun on their faces, looking into the sky. They took a taxi to dinner at the Osteria di Santo Spirito, which Margaret had read about in the guidebook, and drank wine and talked about their day.

When they returned to the del Santos' apartment, late, after dinner, the streets were still crowded with people, the night had turned soft and warm for early April.

"It's so alive," Margaret said, "as if there's too much to see and do and talk about to go to bed."

"I wish we could stay up all night, just go to a café and look at people," Franny said.

"Aren't you tired?"

"Not really."

"I'm exhausted even though today turned out to be surprisingly sweet." She brushed the hair out of Franny's face with her long fingers. "You know, it could have been awful at Ferragamo's. I was afraid it might be awful for you," Margaret said, sinking onto the bed, fully clothed. She covered her eyes with her arm. "You need to go to bed, darling. Tomorrow Signor Ferragamo fits you with a last."

"I can't sleep," Franny said, turning off the overhead light in the bedroom, leaving only the small light on beside her bed.

"And I can't stay awake any longer unless that child starts wailing again," her mother said. "Why don't you read?"

But Franny had no intention of reading.

She sat on top of the blankets fully clothed, waiting, and when Margaret Hall's breathing had deepened to little sighs, she slipped out of the room.

Down the hall, she could hear the del Santos talking and she stood just outside the door to her bedroom listening.

The sounds of Ana Maria whimpering were coming from the next room. The bathroom was just beyond it. If the del Santos happened to catch her opening the door, she could say that she had mistaken Ana Maria's room for the bathroom. Easy enough, she thought, and after all, what was she to think with the sounds coming off and on from that room? What did anyone who stayed in the del Santos' guest room think, and why was this child kept a secret?

Quietly, she went over to the door to Ana Maria's room and turned the knob. The door was locked but there was resistance in the knob when she tried to turn it as if someone were holding on. When she dropped her hand, the knob continued to turn back and forth, faster and faster, and then there came a kind of animal moan like the sound she had once heard coming from the Buckleys' dog when he'd been hit by a car on College Street.

She headed quickly toward the bathroom, as if that had been her destination in the first place, passing Signora del Santo on the run down the hall.

The light from the kitchen spread into the corridor, illuminating an expression of alarm on Signora's face.

Franny ducked into the bathroom as if with purpose, locking the door, waiting until she heard the footsteps pass by.

But the footsteps didn't come.

She waited on the open toilet seat where she sat, fully dressed, but there was no sound, no sound even from the kitchen where people had been talking and laughing.

She washed her face, her hands, splattered her hair with cold water and ran her fingers through it.

And then she opened the door.

Signora del Santo was standing in the hall, a tall woman, very thin with a pretty face, but hardened as if her face were baked clay.

"Come!" she said, indicating the kitchen. "We have a party."

Signor del Santo was sitting at the kitchen table, his feet up on a chair eating a pear. Cheese and crusty bread and brown pears were on a long tray on the table.

Leaning against the stove, where a pot smelling of tomatoes was simmering, was the young man from the café that morning.

"Wine?" Signor del Santo asked. "Would you like wine?"

"No thank you," Franny said although she did want wine.

"No wine," he said to everyone.

"Oh yes, Uncle Mario, our visitor will have wine in honor of this occasion at our house."

The young man spoke English.

Franny could feel the blood rushing to her face, and smiled in spite of her reserve.

He poured a glass of wine and passed it across the table.

"*Salute,*" he said. "I am Filippo del Santo and this you know already is my uncle and aunt."

"I saw you today at the café," Franny said.

"Yes, and I saw you too with your mother. Very nice," he said.

The sound of his name rolled off her tongue like cream.

Filippo del Santo.

Signora del Santo was saying something to the men in Italian, saying it crossly.

"I will translate," Filippo del Santo said. "My aunt and uncle have a daughter called Ana Maria and at night she must be locked in her room for her own protection. I will tell you more sometime later."

"I tried to get in her room by accident, thinking it was the bathroom," Franny said. "Now I know and it won't happen again."

She was drinking wine too quickly out of nervousness and it rushed to her head, thinning her brain, her legs suddenly spaghetti.

"No worry." Filippo was smiling at his uncle. "No worry, yes, Uncle Mario?"

"*Sì,*" Mario agreed, offering more wine.

"Sit down here with me," Filippo said. "I will practice my English."

Franny slipped into a chair next to him.

"Cheese or pears?" He pushed the plate toward Franny. "Pears are excellent."

He cut a slender piece of cheese and pear, putting the cheese on the slice of pear, reached across the table, and put it in Franny's mouth.

"Good, yes?" Filippo asked.

"Lovely," Franny said, getting up from the table. It was time to leave and she was perhaps light-headed with wine, or perhaps with a kind of power that had risen in Florence with this family, with this young man. She was alone, unobserved, and for the first time in her life, she felt equal to the possibilities.

"I should go," she said, the image of Filippo del Santo leaning over to put a piece of pear in her mouth still in her mind. Nothing so intimate had ever happened to her.

Margaret Hall was awake when Franny, woozy with wine, came in the room.

She was reading a Danish novel. She often read books in Danish and it pleased Franny, the Danishness of her mother.

"Where have you been?"

Franny checked her face in the mirror over the dresser to see if it had broken out with nerves.

"That man we saw at the café, you remember?"

"The pretty boy with a newspaper?"

"That one," Franny said. "Filippo del Santo."

"Lucky you. A romance in Florence."

"Not exactly a romance," Franny said. "He was in the kitchen with his aunt and uncle and we talked. That's all."

"Still nice, darling. I always like a possibility in my life."

Franny slipped out of her clothes, into her pajamas, and climbed into bed.

"What do you mean by possibility?" Franny asked.

"Just something that makes me feel hopeful, as if good things might happen."

Franny had an urge to tell her mother about the pear — that Filippo had put a slice of pear with cheese in her mouth just now. That she could still taste it. That he'd reached over and with his fingers had popped it into her mouth as if she and Filippo had known each other always.

It had seemed like the most natural thing in the world but when Franny thought about it later, over and over again, she wondered whether she should have said, "No. No pears."

At first Franny couldn't fall asleep, her mind spinning with the day, with the evening in the del Santos' kitchen, with Filippo, and then she must have dozed off because she awoke in the middle of the night to a commotion.

First she heard Signora del Santo's footsteps running down the corridor from her bedroom next to the kitchen, and then a shattering scream, and Signor del Santo just outside her door, "Shhh, Shhh, Shhh." Maybe to Signora, maybe to Ana Maria.

And then silence.

"Mama." She touched her mother's hand in the dark.

"I heard," Margaret Hall said. "We should move to another pensione tomorrow morning and leave the del Santos to their privacy."

"Why?" Franny asked.

"Because our arrival seems to have caused some alarm."

"Maybe the child is always like this. They rent out rooms so they must be used to it."

"It's beginning to make me feel uncomfortable," Margaret said.

"Filippo is going to explain to me what's the matter with the child next time I see him."

"In the meantime, I won't be sleeping at all."

"Sorry," Signora del Santo said when Franny and her mother stopped by the kitchen to say good morning.

"Sorry for noise," Signor del Santo said. "We give medicine."

"No problem," Margaret Hall said. "We're just on our way to the café for breakfast."

"Please forgive," Signora said. "No more noise."

"It's fine," Franny said. "It didn't bother us."

She looked around for Filippo but he seemed to have left.

They walked down the tilting narrow steps to the courtyard, across the courtyard to the café, and ordered muddy coffee and croissants. Margaret Hall picked up a newspaper in Italian and Franny read the English guidebook they had purchased at the station.

"Can you read Italian?" Franny asked.

"I can *sense* it. I grew up speaking French and English and Danish. So French helps because it's also a Romance language."

She pointed out a photograph of a painting by Michelangelo on the front page of the newspaper.

"I know without speaking Italian that something has happened to this painting by Michelangelo — and I guess that it was either stolen from a church in Rome or damaged," she was explaining as Filippo del Santo wandered into the café, picked up a newspaper, ordered a coffee, and drank it quickly at the bar, stopping by their table as he left.

"So today you see Salvatore, yes?" Filippo asked. "My aunt tells me that you have an appointment with Salvatore for new shoes. He makes very nice shoes. Expensive."

"We do have an appointment with Signor Ferragamo," Margaret said.

"He is my father's cousin. Very good man. Very famous."

Filippo pulled an empty chair from another table and sat down between them.

"Mind if I sit with you?"

"Not at all." Margaret folded the newspaper in her lap.

"So I tell you something, yes?"

"Please," Margaret said.

"I am a painter although very young. Only seventeen." He pushed his chair back, resting it on two legs. "And you?" he asked Franny.

"My age?"

He nodded.

"Almost fifteen," she said, which was almost true.

"Fifteen is good," Filippo said, resting his chin in his hand, looking so directly at Franny that she turned away.

"I was thinking, maybe I could paint you," he said. "You have excellent bones."

"Oh?" Franny said, awkward with such attention.

"Mainly, I paint landscapes of Firenze."

He pointed to the other side of the foundling hospital.

"I paint outside in the hills of Firenze, looking over the city at the tops of things. But now I'm taking a class at my academy for painting the figure and you have a face that is different than all the faces in Firenze." He paused as if he were thinking of a word. "A precise face. I like that very much."

"That's very nice of you," Margaret Hall said, chillier than she usually was. "But we'll only be in Florence for another day or two and then to Rome and home."

"That is agreeable. It doesn't take long to draw the idea of a face. Two hours would be fine. Do you maybe have two hours?"

"I do," Franny said quickly. "This afternoon after I see Ferragamo."

"Good," Filippo said. "You come to my studio which is there." He pointed across the courtyard. "Third floor. There is a doorbell."

He got up to leave.

"You were going to tell us about the del Santos' little girl."

"Yes, you are right. She has brain damage from falling out the window when she was a baby and they keep her hidden. But you will see her. Only they will not take her outside to public view."

"Because of how she looks?" Franny asked.

"She looks very beautiful but she cannot talk, cannot hear. Only scream," he said again. "She is not normal."

"Very sad," Franny said.

"Sometimes if you are different than other people, they don't like you, you know?" he said, returning the chair he had borrowed.

"I do know," Franny said, and she wondered, had he noticed that she was different, and was he being abnormally kind to her because he felt sorry.

"So later, you will let me draw your face, yes?"

"Yes," Franny said. "I'll ring the bell."

"The answer is no," Margaret Hall said after he had gone. "He is not going to draw your face in his studio this afternoon."

Franny thrust her hands in the pockets of her coat and walked toward the river, just ahead of her mother.

They walked along the front, the river splashing against the banks, cars and cycles whipping by the narrow sidewalks, the air dank with exhaust.

"Just my face?" she asked. "Not exactly dangerous."

"He's a stranger and I'm not sure about him."

"I *am* sure."

"You don't know anything about him, Franny."

"I know he's been sweet to me," she said.

"What you don't know about artists is this,"

Margaret Hall began. "Models for artists in figure classes are nude because the artist is learning about the body."

"You can be sure that I won't be nude," Franny said crisply. "He is drawing my face."

Franny walked ahead along the crowded sidewalk, damp from the river heavy in the air, conscious of her mother behind her, but solitary as if a thread between them had been snipped.

She knew she was right. Filippo del Santo was only interested in her face.

Their appointment with Signor Ferragamo was early, before the clients and models arrived, so the Halls would have the showroom to themselves.

Signor Strolla opened the door, even less friendly than the day before.

"Nine o'clock on the dot," he said. "Very early."

He ushered them to the velvet couch in the center of the room, set at an angle so Franny could see herself in profile. She had dressed carefully that morning, choosing a full plaid skirt even though it made her hips look larger and a tight white angora sweater and kneesocks. It was still cool enough in Italy in the morning for wool clothes.

Signor Strolla brought a silver tray of sparkling water in wine glasses and small cookies in the shape of stars on a silver dish. Behind him, a model with short hair, cropped close to her head like a black cap, a taupe wool skirt gathered at the waist, and a white silk shell, followed, stopping at the couch where Franny and her mother were sitting.

"Signor Ferragamo arrive soon," Signor Strolla said, setting the tray down and turning, his leather soles snapping against the marble as he crossed the room and disappeared.

The model smiled. *"Buongiorno!"* she said, and raising her arms slowly in a wide arch like a ballerina, she pointed to the shoes she was wearing. They were black patent pumps with a beige toe, a low square heel on which she turned, lifting the toe off the ground.

"For you, Signorina, new shoes. Very beautiful for girls."

And then she walked across the marble floor following Signor Strolla's steps and through the mirrored door.

"She doesn't shave under her arms?" Franny asked. "All that curly hair and she puts her arms in the air like she's proud of it."

Margaret Hall laughed.

"It's the custom in Europe. Women don't necessarily shave under their arms. It's considered sexy and normal."

"Normal?"

"Normal," her mother said. "What did you think of the shoes she was modeling?"

"Not pretty!"

The model had returned with a new pair of shoes, baby doll flats in soft black leather with round toes and a tiny pink grosgrain ribbon in the middle.

"I love those," Margaret said. "More girly."

"I like them better," Franny said.

"It's good?" the model asked.

"Yes," Franny said. "Very good."

The model slipped out of the room again, and Franny found her mind falling into a scene of a dance in Easterbrook, the big spring dance held at the Knights of Columbus Hall decorated with pastel paper flowers, the dance floor painted blue as if the dancers were moving across the surface of a lake.

Franny was walking into the dance late, after the music had started, wearing a pale pink strapless with a full skirt to her calf and the black baby doll shoes with a pink ribbon to match the dress.

In her daydream, she stopped at the refreshment table, took a cup of Jell-O juice with ginger ale, and, leaning against the table, sipping her drink, she assessed the dancers. Eleanor had arrived in a brown dress, a little too tight at the top, her hair frizzed. She was alone without Mikey.

"Oh jeez, Franny," she'd say in honest surprise. "You look so pretty."

In the corner, Boots was sitting in her confirmation look-alike dress. Franny's friends from elementary school were rushing over, excited to see her, happy at how confident she had become since her trip to Italy.

Behind her, Filippo del Santo, visiting from Florence, slipped his arm around her waist.

Signor Ferragamo sat on a stool beside the couch.

A *last*, he explained, was like a pattern for a dress. If you have a pattern, you can make many, many dresses from that pattern. He drew around her feet on a piece of butcher paper on the floor. And then he measured the length and width of her feet, following the lines of the little crippled toes.

"We will straighten these toes inside the shoe so they will flatten out and not stick up and still feel fine," he said. "And then we will turn the shoe so it leans a little inward and you can walk flat and straight."

He pulled gently at her toes, trying to straighten them, determining how straight he could make them to fit inside the shoes. He put his hand on the floor and asked her to stand on it with one foot, moving his hand this way and that to check how it would feel for the foot if his hand were a shoe. He had her stand and walk barefoot away from him and then back, checking her balance, checking the lift on the orthopedic shoes she always wore, checking the undeveloped leg, measuring its circumference.

Each time he gave Franny a new task, he would enclose her hand in both of his and tell her she was an angel.

"There," Signor Ferragamo said finally. "We are done. All you need to do now is choose lovely shoes in magazines and send me a picture and I will make them for you."

And he lifted her feet in his hands and laid them on his knee.

It was midmorning when they left the Ferragamo showroom and walked along the river, their shoulders brushing, their eyes half closed against the brightness of the sun. They crossed the glittering square of the Uffizi and took a table in an open café.

"You don't think I'll see Signor Ferragamo again?"

"I don't know that. He lives a long way from us."

"I'd like to give him something, then," Franny said. "A present to thank him."

They sat at the café for a while with a coffee and cookies, silent with each other, a kind of sweet sadness in the air, and Franny wasn't sure whether the sadness came from her mother or the day itself or that they were leaving soon to go back to Easterbrook.

She was homesick not for home but for this place that she was leaving. Not only Florence or Signor Ferragamo or even Filippo del Santo, who grew larger and larger in her imagination.

"You know, Mama," Franny said, taking the last cookie from the plate of cookies they had ordered. "I like myself better here than I did in Easterbrook, so I have this lonely feeling about leaving."

"I understand that," Margaret said.

Franny rested her chin in her hands.

"I guess I can take the self I like back to Easterbrook with me, can't I?"

"Of course," her mother said. "You don't need to leave it here."

A waiter came bringing Margaret another coffee, a ham sandwich, and a sweet, and Franny checked her watch.

"I'm going to Filippo's studio now," Franny said finally, finishing her coffee.

Margaret Hall took out a cigarette, tapped it on the table, and lit it.

"He said it would take a couple of hours to draw my face. I could meet you at the pensione."

"I was thinking we'd go out for the rest of the day, maybe on a bus trip to Fiesole."

"I don't want to go to Fiesole."

"That's fine," her mother said. "We will do *something* depending on what we decide when you come back."

She settled into her chair, put her feet on the chair which Franny had left, and took a Danish novel out of her satchel.

"If you actually do get back in two or three hours, then we can make a plan."

"I'll be back," Franny said. "Nothing is going to happen to me."

Her mother shrugged and opened the book in her lap.

"I'll wait for you here," she said. "And Franny, be careful."

LINE DRAWING

Franny walked along the Arno, turning left away from the river on her way back to the piazza where Filippo del Santo's studio was located.

At a café near the Duomo, she stopped for more coffee. *"Caffè con latte,"* she said, standing up at the bar, one foot on the brass railing in the manner of the other customers. She reached into her backpack for lire.

She needed ammunition to meet Filippo in his studio. A bathroom so she could look at herself in the mirror to check whether her face had broken out, whether her hair was full and framed the excellent bones of her face.

Excellent bones. Her father remarked on her good bones, but Franny had always believed he was desperately searching for something complimentary to say about her looks and *bones* was all that came to mind.

Now a stranger, a painter in search of a subject had noticed her bones and remarked on their excellence.

"Bathroom?" she asked the man behind the counter and he pointed to the back of the café.

The room was dark even with the light on, so it was difficult to assess her face, even the way her hair fell around it down to her shoulders, but she was pleased with what she saw. She was prettier than she had been yesterday, last week, just that morning before she left the del Santos'. Odd, she thought, how a face can change in no time at all.

Filippo answered the doorbell in seconds as if he had been waiting for Franny at the top of the stairs, two long flights of them, to the third-floor studio where he worked on his landscape paintings in a tiny room flooded with light.

"I go to Fiesole and look at Firenze from on high," he said to Franny. "And then I go to this window and paint what I see."

She followed him to the window.

"And there I see the beautiful Duomo and the bronze doors of Ghiberti — we will go look at them. Real doors, you see."

He opened a drawer and took out some drawings in pencil.

"In art, you need to reproduce reality first, so I must learn to draw the human body," he said. "But what I love is the human face."

He spread the drawings over the wooden table in the middle of the room.

"Now you see. These are in order, all my work in this class since last September."

There were nudes — many of them of one man, short, skinny, long spaghetti arms, and in the drawings he was standing or lying on his side or holding his head with his hand, sitting on a table with his legs dangling, cross-legged.

"You have to see the muscles and the bones and what happens to the body when you bend or sit or stand or lie."

"Why is there only one man?"

"He is a model and paid for doing this. Also one woman."

He opened another box and took out a set of drawings of a woman with long hair, fleshy with a plump belly, a long nose, and flat cheeks.

Franny knew nothing about art, nothing about drawing. She had no inclination whatever to reproduce what she saw. But the idea of an ordinary person going into a class of students, taking off his clothes and lying or standing or sitting for hours while students examined his nakedness in detail, was as foreign to Franny as the Italian language.

"Do you know these people? I mean personally, like friends."

"No, I don't know them. They are only models and we draw them."

He reached over and touched her chin.

"What I like about your face is the cheekbones, high like little mountains, and your eyes, so far apart and large, not like the Italian women I know with eyes closer together and Madonna faces, especially in Firenze."

Franny slipped into a chair, breathless and dizzy. Maybe it was the wine the night before or her meeting with Ferragamo or maybe the attention to her face, something she had never imagined, and even now could not believe, that this young, handsome man would have such an interest in her ordinary face.

No one in Easterbrook had ever noticed.

"So," Filippo del Santo said. "You sit there and I will make a sketch."

He pulled over a stool, situated Franny so she was directly in front of him, the light on her face, her feet on the rungs of the stool, her hands in her lap. He ran his finger gently down her spine.

"Sit straight," he said. "Don't move. I want a full-on face."

"Smiling?"

"Natural," he said.

"Not smiling then," she said.

"You don't smile?"

"If I try I feel self-conscious."

She watched him, the way his hands moved across the sketch paper, the way he looked at her, a thoughtful expression as though he actually was considering Franny as a person, as a girl, a young woman.

He worked quickly, his fingers flying. He didn't erase. When he had finished, he pushed the sketchbook across the table in her direction.

"Now look," he said.

She looked.

The girl she saw was *herself* — she could recognize that — but it was an exaggerated replication, her eyes larger on the page than she remembered them, her hair darker.

This girl in pencil was actually beautiful, something Franny had never seen when she looked in the mirror.

"What do you think?" Filippo asked.

"Is that how I look to you?" she asked.

"Oh exactly, exactly. Except this eye." He pointed to the left eye. "I cannot quite get this eye right. Your eye is right on center and this one is a little crooked, you see?"

"It looks okay."

"I'll fix it so it's perfect."

She got off the stool, ran her fingers through her long hair, shaking it so it fell full around her face.

"Do I get to have a copy of this drawing?"

"First I need it to make a painting. I'm going to make a painting of you just like this. You will be in a chair. Maybe I'll add a book in your lap and you'll be wearing something red to go with your black hair."

At the Duomo, Filippo showed her the mosaics, telling her about the dome and what it meant and how the light came through the stained-glass windows. They stopped to look at the scenes from the Bible on Ghiberti's bronze doors and wandered the back streets fanning from the Duomo's piazza.

At first she wondered, did Filippo know that she was crippled? Had he noticed or was he so concerned with faces that he didn't see her as she was?

She wanted to ask him in self-defense in case he suddenly said, "What *happened* to you?" But maybe he had noticed and it made no difference. Maybe it was of no more interest to him than if she'd had red hair instead of black. She looked the way she looked and that was agreeable to Filippo del Santo.

"Only some hours until you meet your mother and I have my drawing class," Filippo said. "So I will show you now the heart of Firenze. Not buildings. Buildings you can look at in a book."

They weaved in and out of the pedestrian traffic on the narrow streets, among the people chattering back and forth in Italian, the slender ancient houses, a blue, blue sky spread like an umbrella over their heads.

An older woman stopped them — white haired and small with a wicker basket hanging on her arm full of fruit and artichokes and a small yellow kitten.

"Filippo, Filippo," she said, taking his face in her hands, kissing him on the lips.

"My grandmother," Filippo said and then, after he spoke to his grandmother in Italian, she reached up and kissed Franny on the cheek, laying her face against one of Franny's cheeks and then the other.

Filippo laughed in response to something she had said to him.

"She asked are you my girlfriend? And I said yes and so she kissed you because now you are in our family."

"But I'm going home tomorrow," Franny said.

"But it is today and you are my real girlfriend today."

Filippo's grandmother took a mango from her basket and handed it to Franny.

"She's my father's mother."

They wandered across a piazza with its modest fourteenth-century church and bell tower ringing a familiar melody.

"Three o'clock chimes," Filippo said.

The church was surrounded by small shops and kiosks selling religious trinkets, crucifixes, pictures of the Pope and Jesus, bookmarks, and coins with the figures of saints. Franny picked up a child-size crucifix, fingering the beads.

"Are you Catholic?" Filippo asked.

"I'm nothing," Franny said. "But we live next door to the Episcopal church. That's the most I know about church."

"It's worth it to be a little Catholic for the music and the chanting and incense and the wine at communion. That's what I like about Roman Catholicism although I am supposed to also like the Pope and all the rules for behavior."

"I don't know if my parents even believe in God.

My father is a doctor and he believes in science, and my mother is a rebel and I think what she believes in is human beings although I've never asked her."

"Religion is like dinner in my family. I never had a choice."

He stood in a circle of sun, looking up at the simple rectangular bell tower so different from the brilliance of the bell tower of the Duomo.

"So this is my church. We should go in."

He took her hand.

"You have a scarf?" he asked.

"A scarf?"

"A woman has to cover her head in the church or the priests will ask you to leave."

He took the long turquoise scarf draped like a stole around his neck and put it over Franny's head.

She followed him inside the beige Tuscan stone church, wooden pews, no decoration except a wood-carved Christ, his head hanging, his chin resting on his bony chest, nailed to a slender cross and hanging above the pulpit.

It was cold inside the church and Franny wrapped Filippo's scarf around her shoulders, feeling chosen to have been invited inside Filippo's church, to be wearing his scarf.

A young woman was coming out of a simple black box, large enough for two people, the priest and the confessor.

"A confession box," Filippo said. "Have you seen one?"

"We have St. Bernadette's Catholic Church in Easterbrook where I live but I've never seen a confession box there."

"You know what they're used for?"

"I think I do," Franny said.

"You go into this little box and there's a priest on the other side and you confess your sins to him."

"My friend Boots is very Catholic so I suppose she does that. She's just never mentioned it," Franny said.

"I go almost once a week."

"You have that many sins?"

"I have sins, but not so many," he said. "I go because it is important and makes me think about sin."

"I don't think I ever think about sin," Franny said.

"That is too bad," he said but he was smiling.

Franny had never had so personal a conversation with anyone except her mother.

Maybe this was what it meant to fall in love. Not the silliness of her crush on Mikey Houston talking about nothing in the cafeteria line, but a real conversation. She wanted to know Filippo del Santo's life. She wanted to tell him hers.

"You see that woman?" Filippo was saying.

A curtain separated the confessor from the public, and the young woman had pulled back the curtain and was walking up to the front pew where she sat and knelt.

"That is Maria Denasi."

"You know her too?"

"I know many people in this part of Firenze because I am on the streets, painting or wandering to look at things, and here is where I went to school at the academy and where I have lived for three years."

He pulled back the black curtain of the confession box.

"Do you want to see the inside?"

"Has the priest left?"

"He is gone. He comes, he listens to a confession, he goes."

Franny peered inside, at the seat where the confessor sat, at the sliding door that the priest opened to hear the confession of sins, just a part of his face showing, maybe only his chin and lips, or only his eyes and those in darkness.

"I wanted to be a priest, like most boys growing up in Italy, but then I changed my mind," he said, walking to the front of the church where Maria Denasi was still kneeling. "When I was young, what I liked about becoming a priest was the costume and the power."

"What kind of power?" Franny asked.

"The power to forgive Maria Denasi her sins. Like this." He assumed the posture of a priest, his hands folded, his ear turned toward the space in the confession box. "She goes into confession, a widow, only twenty-four years old with an old husband who has died leaving her with no babies. And the listening priest gets to hear Maria's confession and he can see her beautiful face and know her secrets."

"Why didn't you become a priest then?"

"Because in time I want a woman in my bed with me and children and that can't happen if you're a priest."

Maria stood from her prayers, bowed to the altar, nodded to Filippo, and walked out of the church, her heels clicking along the stone floor.

"Maybe she is pregnant. Maybe she has stolen a scarf from the kiosk or lied to her mother," Filippo said, shrugging. "Who knows? Only the priest."

"That is a lot of power."

They walked out into the sunlight, across the piazza, stopping for a raspberry gelato, leaning against the wall of a building, licking their ice cream. The sun was beginning to sink behind the buildings. Almost four o'clock.

"One more thing I want you to see. We have time."

They crossed the street, in the direction of the river, walking single file on the narrow sidewalk until they reached the bridge.

"We're going to a shop, not on the Ponte Vecchio. Too many tourists. This is a real shop only Italians know. You will like it."

They walked along the front, almost the same height. He held her hand.

"Are you an only child?" Franny asked.

"I am not. I have many brothers but I am the oldest and my parents live in a very small village in Umbria. They sent me here to live with the del Santos and go to the academy for painting."

"Are you homesick living away from your family?" Franny said.

"Oh no. The del Santos are also family. Besides, I am a happy person. I like to look at things, to talk to people, to do my work and help my uncle with his pensione. And I love Firenze."

"I would like to come back," Franny said. "Maybe to live."

"You will be back," Filippo said. "Of course you will be back. I will insist."

The shop was a tiny hole-in-the-wall on the other side of the river, up a long, dusty hill, down some steps into a cave lit by candles, smelling of incense.

No one could have come upon it by accident.

Lia was the proprietor. She sold jewelry that she made herself and material that she wove in silk in the colors of Tuscany, taupe and tangerine and mustard and raisin, colors of the earth.

"We come to Lia for special presents, never to the Ponte Vecchio."

Lia poured a glass of something very hot that flew straight to Franny's head when she drank it. She cut up pomegranates, squeezing the tiny seeds.

"You eat and drink," she said. "Then I give you a present."

Lia looked in one of the boxes stacked on the floor of the tiny shop and took out a slender silver bangle, shining it with a cloth.

"It's very beautiful," Franny said. "How much?"

"No cost to you," the woman said. "A present to you from Filippo. He pay when he sell a painting."

She slipped it on Franny's wrist.

"That's what Filippo told. Find something beautiful for you."

They were on their way to the Uffizi to meet Franny's mother when Filippo kissed her. The street was narrow, only wide enough for a motor scooter and empty of traffic, so they walked in the middle of it.

"Tonight I go to Umbria to visit my parents and tomorrow night when I come back to Firenze, you will be gone."

He stopped in the middle of the winding, narrow street, lifted her chin, and kissed her on the lips.

Four

AN ORDINARY DAY

Franny sat up in bed with a copy of *Mademoiselle* magazine looking at shoes. Next to her on the bed were the letters she was writing to Filippo. Twelve of them so far, eight written on the airplane home, none good enough to send.

When she left for Italy, she had thought that she wanted loafers with a penny in the pocket on the front. Penny loafers were essential among her friends. Most of the models in *Mademoiselle* in casual clothes were wearing them, with or without pennies in the pocket of the shoes. They wore them with jeans and blouses with Peter Pan collars and matching sweater sets and plaid skirts with kneesocks.

But what Franny liked best in the issue of *Mademoiselle* were the ballet flats she had seen on the young women in Florence.

It was very early, before dawn, and the first school day since she'd returned from Italy. Her sense of time was confused. In Easterbrook it was five in the morning; in Rome it was noon, and she was still on Roman time.

Everyone in the house was asleep except Pickle, who was downstairs scratching the furniture, his claws making a bristly sound along the couch, which was his particular favorite. A toilet flushed in her parents' room and she guessed her mother was also up early.

She went downstairs with *Mademoiselle* under her arm and stationery she had bought in Florence. She set the water on for tea, opened the front door and picked up the morning paper, opened the fridge and took out milk for cereal.

Melancholy was what she felt, as if it were the day after Christmas or the last day of summer vacation before school started. Some combination of excitement for what was coming and sadness for what was gone.

She tore a photograph of black ballet slippers on the feet of a young girl in a jumper and turtleneck sweater out of the May *Mademoiselle* to send to Signor Ferragamo.

"Choose three pairs and send the pictures in the mail to me," he had suggested.

Three seemed excessive to Franny since she had never, except for the doomed silver shoes, had more than two pairs of shoes, her frequently refurbished orthopedic monsters, one black, one brown.

∽◉∾

On their last night in Florence, Franny and her mother had come home early after a quick dinner around the corner from Ferragamo's showroom. Just as they were sitting down in the café in a table next to the window, Franny, watching the street traffic, thinking of Filippo, saw Signor Ferragamo hurry by the window wearing brown trousers and a sweater, his thin hair lifted in the light wind and drizzle.

She could run after him, easily catch up to him, but what would she say except another good-bye, another thank-you, maybe a double kiss on each cheek, and so she simply watched as he rushed ahead and disappeared in the crowd of shoppers.

She had thought that she might tell her mother about Filippo del Santo but she did not. Maybe later at home she might say he had kissed her on the street as they were walking. Maybe not.

Ana Maria del Santo was in the kitchen on her mother's lap when Franny and her mother got back to the pensione to pack for an early departure. She was small, maybe three or four years old, with long black curly hair and round dark eyes, one flat without expression.

She reached out her arms to Franny.

"You want to hold?" Signora del Santo asked.

The child wound her arms around Franny's neck so tight she had to release them, and she felt the child's heart pounding like drums against her chest.

Later, back in their room at the pensione, their suitcases packed, gifts they had bought stuck in little corners around their clothes, Franny retrieved the silver bracelet she had gotten for Eleanor from her suitcase.

"I'd like to give Ana Maria a gift," she said, heading back to the kitchen where Ana Maria was dozing in her mother's lap, Signor del Santo putting supper on the table.

"I have a present for Ana Maria."

"You like Ana Maria?" Signora del Santo asked.

"Oh yes, she is beautiful," Franny said.

Tears came to Signora del Santo's eyes.

"You say Ana Maria is beautiful," Signor del Santo said. "It make my wife happy and she cry."

"Will you say good-bye to my baby?" Signora asked.

"I would like to," Franny said.

Signora lifted Ana Maria into Franny's arms.

"You kiss?" she asked.

Franny kissed her sleep-warm cheeks, the top of her head. Then she took the silver bracelet and put it in her chubby hands.

The child giggled, a funny little half giggle back in her throat, and reached out, pushing the silver bracelet in Franny's mouth.

Franny poured cereal and made tea, listening upstairs to hear if it was Zeke who had been walking around on the hardwood floors. She wasn't ready for Zeke's endless questions so early in the morning.

Dear Signor Ferragamo,

I am back in the United States now, in my hometown of Easterbrook, Ohio, and I wouldn't invite you to visit me here because you'd hate it. No one drinks wine. No one has heard of caffè con latte or gelato, and the girls in Easterbrook only wear loafers with pennies in the pocket on top.

So this is the shoe I have chosen, thinking three is too many for the first time. I don't know how the ballet shoes will look with my heavy lift but I'm sure you'll figure out a way to make them look beautiful.

In the meantime, I love Italy and especially Florence and you.

Your friend,
Francine Hall

She reread the letter, crossing out "... and you" which seemed presumptuous, stuck the letter in the envelope, and put it on the kitchen counter for her mother to mail.

The headline on the front page of the Easterbrook paper reported: *President Eisenhower a strong favorite in Ohio for a second term.* Underneath the headline was a photograph of the Easterbrook High baseball team opening its season, Mikey Houston in the front row, number thirty-seven.

Zeke came downstairs in his pajama bottoms, no top, and his red hair, longer than he usually wore it, was wet and combed to the side. He padded barefoot across the linoleum floor and sat down on a chair across from Franny.

"Mama says you are changing your name to Francine," he said.

"It's not a change. That's my real name."

"I don't want to call you Francine."

"You don't have to call me that but it's the name I'm using now. And maybe when you're my age, you'll decide to be called Ezekiel instead of Zeke."

"I won't decide that."

He reached across the table and took a Cheerio from the top of Franny's bowl and put it in his mouth, resting his chin on his hand.

"So now you're going to get a million pairs of shoes like Mama?"

"Not like Mama. But I'll get new shoes."

He went over to the counter and opened the cookie jar, taking out two chocolate chips.

"Want one?"

"I don't."

"Did you know that Mrs. Clifford died when you were in Italy?" Zeke asked.

"No one told me," Franny said, and although she didn't know Mrs. Clifford well or even like her, she had a sudden weakness in her stomach that comes with bad news.

"She died at her house and John Boy in my class got to see her carried out dead because he lives across the street."

He broke his cookie in several pieces, eating only the chocolate chips.

"They carried her out of the house on a stretcher," Zeke said, happy with his story. "John Boy told us about it in Show-and-Tell yesterday."

Franny took a handful of Cheerios out of the box.

"But it isn't so bad because I never liked Mrs. Clifford anyway. She used to yell at me when I rode my bike down Main Street because I was on the sidewalk on her side of the street, but Daddy says we can't speak ill of the dead so I'm not allowed to tell people that."

"It's strange to think of her dead when I saw her on the bus just a couple of months ago."

"I saw her too on Saturday when I was playing at John Boy's and she was in her front yard picking up the paper but I didn't say hi and I feel bad about that."

He leaned into Franny's shoulder.

"What else has happened?" she asked.

"Aunt Estelle called from New York and Dad made me talk to her because he doesn't like to talk on the telephone." He pushed away the milky cereal that Franny had poured into a bowl. "I got to eat whatever I wanted while you were away. One night Daddy let me have potato chips and grape soda for dinner."

"Disgusting," Franny said. "Have you seen Eleanor or Boots?"

"Only Boots at the drugstore having a fight with her father, but I know that Mikey Houston broke up with Eleanor because Aunt Gabbie and Uncle Tom came over for dinner and they told Daddy about it and said that Eleanor is feeling terrible but they're not sorry because Mikey's family is poor."

"Poor is okay. I like Mikey's family."

"Also I didn't tell you, I got the stomach flu and Daddy was so busy with other people's kids that I just had to lie in bed and throw up by myself."

"I'm sure Daddy didn't leave you by yourself with the stomach flu," Franny said, ruffling Zeke's hair.

"He did," Zeke said. "At least he left to go to the hospital when Rufus Jones got hit in the eye with a baseball and that's when I threw up."

"Well, you're fine now, Zekey," Franny said and got up from the table, put her cereal bowl in the sink, and dumped the cereal she'd made for Zeke back in the box. It was time for school and she hadn't even dressed.

Upstairs, her mother's high heels tap, tapped across the hall.

"Did you know Mrs. Clifford died?" Franny asked, meeting her on her way downstairs.

"I did," her mother said.

"Didn't it seem strange that she died while we were away?"

"Mrs. Clifford was an old lady. An old, unpleasant lady."

"I have this crazy feeling that she might not have died if I'd been here."

"That is a crazy feeling, darling, and I don't think you could have kept her alive," Margaret Hall said and she was smiling, a conspiratorial smile.

In her bedroom, Franny shut the door, took clothes for school out of her closet, and sat on the end of the bed.

She pulled on her slacks, a brown turtleneck, socks, and her orthopedic shoes, brushed her hair, and went to her parents' room to borrow makeup. She needed to look more dramatic, she thought, opening the black mascara. After all, she'd been to Italy.

She brushed her hair back in a ponytail, changed to a yellow Peter Pan blouse and put the collar up, a sassy look, she thought. At the last minute, she spread lipstick across her lips so they looked shiny but not too red.

"I have written Signor Ferragamo," she said to her mother, heading downstairs. "If you could address the letter."

"What did you order?" Margaret Hall asked, on the phone with Estelle, her hand across the receiver.

"Not penny loafers," Franny called, grabbing her book bag.

Boots met her unexpectedly at Main and Oliphant, and they walked the rest of the way to school together.

"You're wearing makeup!"

"I am," Franny said. "Cranberry Ice is the name."

"I'm not allowed. Ever, my mother says, until I get married," Boots said. "So I guess you heard Mikey broke up with Eleanor."

"Zeke told me."

"He said he was tired of her. Can you believe that?"

"I can. Boys can be very mean."

"And Mrs. Clifford died." Boots slung her book bag over her shoulder.

"Zeke told me that too. It was the high point of his week."

"Heart failure is what my mother said. She was eighty-four and *boom*, she's dead."

"Eighty-four is pretty old."

They pushed open the heavy doors of the high school and headed to the lockers.

"I'm trying out for cheerleader today. You are too, right?"

"I'm not," Franny said, opening her locker, hanging up her jacket.

"You're not? Every girl in the ninth grade is trying out," Boots said. "Honestly, Franny, it won't make any difference about your feet if that's what you're worried about. You'll probably get elected to the squad without a problem."

"I'm actually not worried about my feet."

She took the books for English and social studies out of her book bag and closed the locker.

"Before I left for Italy I thought I wanted to be a cheerleader and now I just don't think I do."

They walked together to English class and took their seats in the back of the room.

"Did you have a good time in Italy?"

"I did," Franny said. "Very nice."

But she was not ready to talk about it with Boots. It was her own private story and she didn't know how to begin.

She opened her English notebook and wrote at the top of the page.

Dear Filippo, I'm sitting in English literature class with all of my friends from before I came to Italy and met you — Boots and also my cousin Eleanor and her old boyfriend who was also my crush (crush is a boy you dream about but don't have for your very own), Mikey Houston, and all of the other freshmen at Easterbrook High School, and I feel as if I'm wearing one of those veils the Italian women wear to church so that what I see through my veil is washed and blurry.

Nothing here seems real. Not high school and not these friends and their problems with boyfriends or cheerleading or their constant jealousies.

I could move to Italy. I'd need to think of what to do about my mother and my little brother, Zeke. My father couldn't join us because he's a doctor and needed here in Easterbrook but he could visit.

What would you advise?

Yours sincerely, Francine

She crossed out *Yours sincerely* and wrote *Yours truly* which didn't seem exactly right either. So she crossed out *Yours truly* and wrote *Love*.

"So I guess you heard about Mikey," Eleanor said, catching up with Franny after class.

"I did."

"Just like Easterbrook. Everybody in the whole town knows so I walk around as if I've got *DUMPED* hanging around my neck."

"I'm very sorry, Eleanor."

"At least I don't like him any longer, not even his dimples which I used to love. Now when I look at him, I only see pimples."

Boots was in the cafeteria talking to Mikey when Franny walked in.

"I'm not sitting anywhere near them," Eleanor said, getting into the cafeteria line. "I hate them all, everyone in the whole high school."

"So did you get to see the Pope?" Mikey asked.

"He was too busy," Franny said, putting her tray down at the table where Boots was sitting next to Sally Ann Fergusen.

"Well, a lot went on while you were gone. I guess you heard from Eleanor."

"I heard."

"Did you hear that my sister got together with a new boy from Cleveland? And Boots's mom is going to let her get a new dress for the spring dance. Big deal, yeah? No more Catholic virgin outfits at the proms."

"True story," Boots said. "We're going to Cleveland on Saturday, me and my sisters and my mom."

"And also," Mikey went on, "Mr. Garland in history was fired because the principal found him drunk in his car in the high school parking lot on a school day, so he's moved to Akron to live with his mom."

"I saw your picture in this morning's paper," Franny said.

"Yeah. My third time in the paper in a week."

"He was elected co-captain. Pretty amazing for a freshman," Boots said.

"Are you trying out for cheerleading?" Sally Ann Fergusen asked the group, passing around her plate of french fries.

"Who isn't?" Mikey asked.

"Franny says she's not," Boots said.

"Honest to God, you're not?" Sally Ann asked. "How come?"

"I decided against it," Franny said, catching a familiar exchange of *we know why* pass between Sally Ann and Boots.

"The only reason I would have tried out is because it's the thing to do in ninth grade," Franny said, taking a french fry from Sally Ann's plate. "I wouldn't exactly be a very good cheerleader."

On her way home after school, Franny caught up with Eleanor headed to the soda shop.

"I don't know what to do about the spring dance because of Mikey," Eleanor said.

"Just go like you used to do before Mikey."

"Are you going?"

"I honestly don't know how I feel about the dance," Franny said. "Even if the new shoes I get are perfect, I may not want to go."

"Me neither," Eleanor said, "and I don't even need to worry about shoes."

Ahead on Scioto Street, Zeke was dragging his book bag, walking alone.

"I'm glad you're back in America," he said when she had caught up with him.

"I'm glad to see *you*," Franny said.

"Well, another thing I didn't tell you happened while you were away is Joey Ferris beat me up on the playground. He squished my face into the dirt so I could hardly breathe."

"When did that happen?"

"On last Thursday while you were gone," Zeke said. "I didn't like it that you guys were in Italy. It would have taken you days to get back if I'd been really hurt."

"I'm hugely sorry, Zeke."

She reached down and took his hand.

"Daddy's a little mean to me when Mama's not here," he said, leaning against her arm.

On the front porch, Margaret Hall in blue jeans and a sweater was reading the paper, her feet up on the railing.

"So how was your day?" she asked.

"Mine was terrible," Zeke said. "Joey Ferris beat me up on the playground and pushed my face in the dirt."

"Zeke," Franny said. "I thought that happened on Thursday while we were gone."

"But you guys weren't here so it feels like it happened again," Zeke said, picking up Pickle.

"I've already called Joey Ferris's mom, and she felt terrible about it and Joey is going to be punished. Hours of punishment. He'll probably have to stay in his room for a week," Margaret said.

"Good," Zeke said.

"I told her what Joey did was unacceptable."

"Unacceptable is right," Zeke said, carrying Pickle in the house.

Franny sat down on a wicker chair next to her mother.

"What about you?" Margaret asked.

"It was fine. Normal," Franny said. "Nothing's changed since we've been gone. All the conversations were the same ones we had before I left."

"This is a very small town, darling."

"I guess it is."

"Did you tell everyone about Italy?"

Franny put her feet up on the railing next to her mother's.

"I had thought I would tell them. I even had conversations in my head about what I would say, but when I got to school, I wanted to keep Florence to myself," Franny said. "It felt as if what happened belonged to me and no one would exactly understand."

It had started to rain, a soft early April rain, wind blowing across the porch, misting their faces with cool water.

THE LOVELY SHOES

The shoes arrived by ship from Italy in the middle of May, a week before the spring dance. They were on the front porch on a Friday afternoon when Franny got home with Boots, who had made the cheerleading squad, announced that afternoon.

Franny saw the package as they walked up the front steps and she knew what it was, but she didn't want Boots to be there when she opened the shoes for the first time, so she left them where they were by the door.

The mail was on the table in the front hall — she checked it first thing every afternoon. There were bills for her parents, a letter from Aunt Estelle, an invitation, probably to Sally Ann's birthday party, and a postcard from Zeke's friend Peter in Cleveland. Nothing from Filippo. It was the eighteenth of May. She had been back in Easterbrook for almost a month and still she had not heard from Filippo.

She had written him more than thirty letters, which she kept in a box in the second drawer of her desk, writing every night before she turned out the light. She kept the bracelet he had given her in the same drawer with the letters, telling herself she'd wear it when he wrote. Then she'd wear it *if* he wrote. Pretty soon she would wear it whether he wrote or not.

But only one letter, the first one she had written, had been sent. It was a formal letter thanking Filippo for the afternoon they spent together and giving him her home address.

"So I'm glad Sally Ann Fergusen made the squad," Boots was saying, "although I thought Amanda would be elected and Ellen Cross, but I'm really surprised about Eleanor because she's so pudgy. You know what I mean? She doesn't exactly look like a cheerleader."

"She's cute. Cheerleaders are supposed to be cute," Franny said, pouring milk, searching in the cookie jar for chocolate chips among the lemon cookies.

"And what did you think about Meg Austin? I thought she'd make it and then she didn't and she was crying her eyes out in the girls' room. I said I was sorry and she couldn't even talk." Boots flopped down on a kitchen chair. "So you must be glad you didn't try out since it's awful if you don't make it."

Franny put an Elvis LP on the record player, turning the volume low since her mother was upstairs working on a drawing of the brain for a neurological journal.

"It's so crazy, Franny," Boots said, wiggling to Elvis while she talked. "We've been best friends since third grade and you're still my best friend, but ever since we started high school, I can't tell what matters to you. Like being a cheerleader. I *know* you wanted to be a cheerleader earlier this year — and then *POOF*, it didn't matter."

"That's true. I changed my mind."

"How come?"

"I don't know," Franny said, lifting Pickle onto her lap.

Ever since she had come back from Italy, she'd felt a kind of ease come over her as if finally she *fit* in her own body.

"But I'm glad for you and Eleanor and Sally Ann."

"Really?" Boots asked, incredulous.

"Really," Franny said.

And it was true.

When Margaret Hall came downstairs, Boots was bubbling over with conversation about the squad and how she had to buy new shoes and pay for the sweater and maybe her mother would be willing to sew the big red *E* on the front of the sweater.

"So the cheerleading squad's been announced?" Margaret asked.

"Boots made it," Franny said. "And Eleanor and Sally Ann."

"That's wonderful." Margaret filled the teapot with tap water. "Who else?"

Boots rattled off the names.

"Only Franny didn't try out," she said.

Margaret made a cup of tea and sat down at the table as Boots was putting on her coat to leave.

"She told me she wasn't going to," Franny's mother said.

"I'm going to Cleveland tomorrow to get a new dress," Boots said. "Do you have one for the dance?"

"I got a periwinkle dress when we went shopping for the Valentine's Dance," Franny said.

"So you'll go to the spring dance?"

"Maybe," Franny said, following Boots to the front door. "Probably."

After Boots left, she picked up the package from Ferragamo's on the front porch and went back into the kitchen.

"A letter came to you today from Italy," Margaret Hall said. "I saw the thin paper and the Italian stamp and thought it was from Signor Ferragamo for me."

She reached into the pocket of her trousers and handed Franny a slim blue envelope.

"Filippo," Franny said.

"Filippo, yes."

Franny took the letter and put it in her backpack, her heart beating in her throat.

"I'd almost given up on him," she said. "It's been a month."

"Aren't you going to read it?"

"Not now," she said. "Not yet. My shoes came."

She put the box on the kitchen table.

"I didn't even notice," Margaret said. "Open it up."

Franny heard her father's footsteps coming across the front porch and he opened the front door, coming into the kitchen, kissing Franny on the top of her head as he used to do when he came home from the hospital but had not done since the summer.

"Your shoes!" he said. "This is very exciting."

Franny got a knife out of the drawer and slit the box open along the line of packing tape.

"I don't know if you'll like the shoes I chose, Daddy,"
she said. "A lot of the Italian girls my age are wearing them.
I saw a picture in one of Mama's fashion magazines."

Franny crossed her fingers, closed her eyes tight, and
took off the top of the box.

"Gorgeous!" her mother said even before the shoes
were out of the box. "Oh, Franny, I'm so excited."

The shoes were soft black leather, a little bow at the
base, flat with a round toe. The left foot shoe with its
high lift that would even out the length of her legs was
remarkably made. Although the lift was obvious to Franny,
it would be difficult for a person looking at Franny with
her shoes on to tell that one shoe was quite so different
from the other.

"Try them on," Margaret Hall said.

Franny leaned over and slipped her right foot easily
into the shoe. Her left foot, however, kept getting stuck
as she pushed it until her mother brought her a shoe horn
and edged the foot into the shoe.

"Beautiful, darling," her mother said. "Walk. Walk
across the room."

And Franny did.

She stood very straight, moving easily side to side,
balancing on the flat of her foot.

"Perfect, Franny," her mother said softly. "Look at them in the mirror on the door."

Franny opened the downstairs closet door with its full-length mirror and looked at her feet, surprised at how small and normal they appeared.

"They're good, aren't they?" she asked her mother about the shoes.

"They're beautiful, Franny."

Her mother made tea, her father made himself an old-fashioned with bourbon and water and a maraschino cherry and turned the news on the television. Franny sat with her mother and talked about Filippo and the workshop at Ferragamo's, about the cheerleading squad and the spring dance.

When Zeke came home after playing at Benji's, tears running down his cheeks because Benji had called him a *bear cub*, Franny grabbed him around the waist and pulled him into her lap.

"My very own fuzzy bear cub," she said as he finished the rest of her cookies.

Upstairs, while her mother cooked dinner, Franny took the thin, crispy letter from Filippo out of the envelope. Behind it folded double was the drawing he had done of Franny, looking very much as she remembered it, only prettier.

Dear Francine,

I am sending the drawing I made of your face. I have now made the painting, which is hanging on the wall of my studio. I have given you blue eyes, striped with yellow which I believe to be the color of your sparkling eyes, and a red sweater just as I said I would. You are beautiful. I will keep this painting forever but I hope you will visit soon, maybe this summer and I can show it to you. Love, Filippo del Santo

She lay very still on her back listening to the banging of pots and pans in the kitchen, her father on the phone with the hospital as usual, the sound of the television which Zeke was watching before dinner.

When her mother knocked to tell her that dinner was ready, Franny slipped Filippo's letter without the drawing in the drawer with her own collection of letters to him which she had never sent.

"Coming," she said, taking the drawing downstairs with her.

Her mother had lit the candles so the dining room was almost dark and it felt very like the trattorias where they had eaten in the evenings in Florence. She had made chicken with olives and artichokes and little potatoes, food she had learned about in Florence.

Beside Franny's place there was a wine glass.

"We're having a celebration of shoes," Zeke said from his place at the table. "You get to drink wine, Franny."

Franny slipped into her chair next to her father, who still had on his suit from the hospital, his medical bag beside him.

"May I have wine for the shoe celebration?" Zeke asked.

Franny's father poured a thimbleful of wine in Zeke's glass.

"To your lovely shoes," Dr. Hall said.

"So are you going to the spring dance, Franny?" Zeke asked. "My friend Jono's sister is in your class and she got a new dress for the dance."

"What do you plan to wear, Franny?" her father asked.

"I don't even know whether I'll go or not," Franny

said, reaching in her pocket to take out the drawing that Filippo had made. "But if I do I'll wear a periwinkle blue dress."

"Eleanor called to see if you'd come to the Knights of Columbus Hall and decorate with her tonight," Margaret said. "She's feeling unhappy about Mikey Houston."

"Of course I'll help decorate," Franny said.

"Mama said you got a boyfriend in Italy," Zeke said.

"I did get a boyfriend," Franny said. "He made a drawing of me."

She unfolded the drawing and handed it to Zeke.

"How come it's just your face?" Zeke asked, taking the drawing and examining it.

"Because he likes my face."

"Your face?"

"Yes, Zekey, he likes my face."

She passed it to her father.

Dr. Hall lifted the candle over the drawing so he could see it better.

"This is beautiful, Franny."

"It's just me, not exactly beautiful," Franny said.

"But it is, darling," her mother said, taking the drawing from Dr. Hall, holding it up so it was backlit by the hanging light in the dining room. "He has captured something wonderful in your face."

"Like what?" Zeke asked.

"Light," Margaret said. "Franny's face is full of light."

Zeke leaned over the picture, his chin in his hand.

"I don't see where the light is," he said.

"Everywhere," Franny said and they all laughed.

Margaret cleared the dishes, blew out the candles.

"I like the blue formal for tomorrow night," she said.

Franny didn't reply. Before she'd left for Italy, the *school dance* had been the map of her failure as a girl with boys.

Now the dance had lost the air in its balloon and become something that Franny could do or not. More or less like every other occasion in high school, birthday parties and movies, trips to Cleveland.

Upstairs in her bedroom, she read Filippo's letter again. She wished he had given her a photograph to put in a frame to keep on her bedside table. She would ask him for one. After all, he had a picture of her in a red sweater in his studio.

"Do you want to try on the dress and shoes together?" her mother called from her bedroom.

"Sure," Franny said, putting the letter back in her drawer.

She slipped on the black ballet slippers, put the periwinkle blue strapless dress over her head.

"Look at yourself in my full-length mirror," her mother said. "You'll be surprised."

It was almost seven, dusk smoking the horizon. The members of St. James Episcopal Church choir were walking past the front window of the Halls' house on their way to choir practice, the church bells ringing the hour. Zeke, his cowboy gun in its holster strapped around his waist, had mounted his imaginary horse and galloped into the bedroom, watching Franny reflected in the mirror.

Margaret Hall was stretched out on the bed in her black trousers and high-heeled strappy shoes, her hair swept up in a loose bun like a movie star.

"What do you think?" her mother asked as Franny stood in front of the mirror.

"I think I look like the girl Filippo del Santo imagined when he saw me."

"Not the girl he imagined, darling," she said. "The girl he saw."

Outside the window, the wind had picked up, whipping the branches against the bedroom window. Zeke galloped his horse over to the window and looked out.

"Do you think it's a tornado?" he asked.

"We don't get tornadoes in Ohio," Franny said, sitting on her parents' bed, settling on the pillow next to her mother, her legs stretched out in front of her, the toes of her ballet slippers barely visible under the periwinkle skirt.

"You know Filippo didn't even notice my legs."

"He noticed *you*, didn't he?"

"I guess he did." Franny smiled, slipping her hand into her mother's, and for a while, until she heard her father coming upstairs to bed, they leaned against the headboard side by side, listening to the sound of the leaves rustling like dancers, watching the lights flicker out in the houses across the street until it was dark.

WHAT IS TRUE

$\mathcal{T}he \mathcal{L}ovely \mathcal{S}hoes$ is an invented story, but some of the things that happen in the book happened to me, although in a different way. When I was eighteen months old, I caught the disease polio, against which children today (and since 1953) are inoculated, and so polio no longer exists in the United States. It is a neurological disease and the form that I contracted paralyzed me for several weeks. Then some of the muscles in my legs returned and some did not. I spent two years living off and on at the Warm Springs Polio Foundation between the ages of eleven and thirteen, having surgeries that made it possible for me to walk and run and, in fact, become a cheerleader, which I certainly wanted to be. Franny is born *crippled* and *crippled* was the word used to describe anyone whose legs didn't work properly or were twisted or deformed in any way. We no longer use that word, considered insulting in our current vocabulary, but growing up I was called a cripple. Nor do we use *gimp*, but I remember absolutely the day in fifth grade when a boy who I still know and then loved called me *gimp*, and I think about that every time I see him now.

There are two incidents in the book true to my own life. My mother bought me regular shoes at G. C. Murphy's, a five-and-ten store, to wear to my first formal dance. Because they didn't fit properly, she stuffed them with toilet paper. While I was dancing with Kirk White, the toilet paper got loose and to my humiliation, it trailed behind my long dress. I headed quickly to the girls' room where I hid out in one of those cubicles with my feet up under my chin so no one would know I was there until the dance was over. And that was my last dance for a very long time.

When I was about fourteen, my mother read a story about Salvatore Ferragamo who in fact did — and his company still does — make beautiful shoes. She wrote Ferragamo a letter and told him about me and my problem at the dance and asked could he make me a pair of shoes. By the time we got to Italy, Ferragamo had died, so I never met him, although in the story, Franny Hall does. But his children made me a last, and for several years, I ordered shoes from pictures in magazines, even the shoes I wore in my wedding, and they came by mail.

I would have continued ordering these lovely shoes had not the factory with the lasts had a fire and my last was destroyed.

And so this book about Franny Hall, who is not me, and Margaret Hall, who is not unlike my mother, owes a great debt to my real mother, who would not stop wishing for lovely shoes for her daughter, and to Salvatore Ferragamo and his lovely family, who made it possible for me to wear shoes that were not stuffed with toilet paper.

Susan Shreve

Susan Shreve
Washington, D.C.

ACKNOWLEDGMENTS

As always, I am so lucky in Arthur Levine for his fierce editorial standards and his child's heart. To the great group at Arthur A. Levine Books and Scholastic—what an honor to be published by you—and to Emily Clement, vigilant, funny, and smart. It goes without saying that my determined, beautiful mother made possible my story, with the generous collaboration of the Ferragamos and their lovely shoes.

This book was art directed and designed by Marijka Kostiw. The jacket photograph was done by Marc Tauss. The text was set in 12-pt. Hoefler Text Roman, a typeface designed by Jonathan Hoefler in 1991. Display type was set in Bickham Script, which was designed by Richard Lipton in 2000 for Linotype. Bickham is based on the lettering of 18th-century writing masters as seen in engravings of George Bickham. Display font was set in Copperplate, designed by Frederic Williams around 1905. The book was printed and bound at R. R. Donnelley in Crawfordsville, Indiana. Production was supervised by Cheryl Weisman, and manufacturing was supervised by Adam Cruz.